NOTHING MORE DECEITFUL

A PRIDE AND PREJUDICE VARIATION

SOPHIA GREY

1

———————

*A*s happened every year, and more times than Elizabeth Bennet liked to think on, Longbourn was filled with noise and chaos while the women of the household prepared for the much anticipated Meryton assembly.

Second only to the Regimental Christmas Ball in its grandeur, even Elizabeth could admit that the September assembly was a welcome diversion from the rapidly shortening days and the loss of summer's warmth. But, as soon as it ended, they would talk of nothing but the next event as though the assembly had not even occurred.

Elizabeth sighed heavily as her younger sister's arguments flowed from the corridor into the parlor.

"Lizzy! Lydia will not listen to me," Kitty moaned as the youngest Bennet sister elbowed her way into the room and left Kitty standing in the doorway.

Elizabeth did not look up from her sewing, but made certain that her irritation could be heard very clearly in her words. "For the very *last* time, Lydia. Kitty will be borrowing my gloves for the assembly tonight," Elizabeth said firmly. "And do not ask if I have changed my mind. I can readily assure you that I have not, and shall not, do such a thing."

Elizabeth caught her sister Jane's disapproving glance, but it could not be helped. Lydia really *was* being difficult, and she deserved Elizabeth's ire.

"You are *so* unkind!" Lydia cried. "You know that they will not look well on Kitty's arms. They are much too short and they will sag at the elbow. It is ever so unfair!"

Lydia crossed her arms over her chest and pouted as Kitty looked down at her arms. "They are not too short," she complained as she pulled the gloves out of Lydia's fist and rubbed her fingers over the embroidery at the edge. The gloves were not special by any means, and that Lydia only wanted them because Kitty would be wearing them... but it did not make her behavior acceptable.

"I promise that I will be ever so careful with them," Kitty said reverently.

Elizabeth sighed heavily and turned her attention back to the hem she was sewing. She was very careful with her things, and it was not often that she was able to purchase new items for her wardrobe, but she could not very well say no when one of the other girls asked to borrow something.

"I know you will take very good care of them," she said with a small smile. "Now *do, please*, both of you, leave this room at once and finish dressing. The carriage will be here to collect us within the hour and Mama will be beside herself if we are not there in time for the opening dances!"

"Mama says that the first dances are the best chance a young lady has of being noticed," Kitty said primly as Lydia pushed her out the door.

"Nonsense," Lydia exclaimed. "The only way to catch the eye of a gentleman is to take every opportunity to dance and be merry in their company!"

"That is not true at all," Kitty cried. "Mama would never approve—"

Elizabeth shook her head and set the final stitch to secure the velvet ribbon to the hem of her own dress for the evening.

"I do not believe that Lydia has calculated how exhausting her plans to garner the attention of the officers might be..." Jane said. Elizabeth could hear the amusement in her sister's voice, but she could not find her own mirth.

"That is certainly clear," she said.

"You do not seem overly excited to attend this assembly, Lizzy," Jane observed. "You are far too melancholy for such an evening..."

Elizabeth laid aside her sewing and tried to smile. Jane might have been teasing her, but she had been feeling out of sorts for the last few days—the way one feels before the breaking of a thunderstorm or after a very hot day—and she could not determine what was the matter.

"I am, as yet, undecided," she replied thoughtfully.

"But this new gentleman," Jane said, "Mr. Bingley. Surely his arrival, and the arrival of his guests would have brought you some cheer? Mama is quite thrilled by the prospect of another gentleman in Meryton. Two or three gentlemen, in fact, if the gossip is correct. Has there been any more news of him?"

Elizabeth frowned slightly. It had been more than a fortnight since the gentleman's arrival in Meryton, and Mrs. Bennet had harangued her husband almost daily to visit Netherfield Park and welcome Mr. Bingley to their society.

Elizabeth had a sneaking suspicion that their father had already done precisely that, but was waiting for his wife to stop asking him about it—something which would never occur.

They could both be equally, and painfully, stubborn at times.

"There has been no other news aside from Mama's

lamentation that every gentleman in Hertfordshire in possession of daughters of marriageable age will have descended upon Netherfield Park to make their greetings and acquaintance. Why, I have heard from Charlotte that her father called upon them not two days after their arrival!"

Jane blinked at her sister incredulously. "So soon?" she gasped.

It was well known that Charlotte Lucas was nearing an age where marriage would seem to be beyond her reach, but such eagerness on Sir William's part could be misconstrued as desperation—no matter how well intentioned.

"I cannot think ill of Charlotte," Elizabeth said. "Goodness knows that the poor girl could benefit from some flattery and attention. And I know she is not responsible for her father's... exuberance."

Jane laughed gently and shook her head. Sir William could, indeed, be infernally excitable, and this would not be the first occasion that he had thrust himself into a perceived social faux pas—and it would likely not be the last. Lady Lucas did an admirable job of diverting attention from her husband's antics and meddling, and Elizabeth could only hope that such things would not affect Charlotte's prospects overmuch.

Charlotte was a practical young woman, but her practicality had prevented her from being as open to change and serendipity as other young women of their acquaintance. Elizabeth was not even certain whether or not Charlotte had any thoughts, of one direction or another, in regards to marriage, for she had never confided any.

Elizabeth had her own wishes for marital bliss, and Jane did as well—but Charlotte Lucas, ever since they had been children together—had remained aloof and uninterested in sharing such things.

"You must help me decide what to wear," Jane said with a frown. "You have re-hemmed that gown beautifully, and now I have doubts in my own choice!"

Elizabeth set her supplies back into her sewing box and draped her gown over her arm. She had been fond of pale pinks lately and had chosen this dress specifically for its color, and for the fact that she had not worn it for some time. It was the color of a cherry blossom in the spring sunshine and reminded her of Longbourn's gardens. The color looked well against her summer-kissed skin and would show prettily under the candlelight that would illuminate the Meryton assembly rooms.

They departed the parlor, leaving Mary to read alone in her chair. Their younger sister had been dressed for the assembly for hours, but she had only done so to avoid the usual flurries of preparation that took up so much time before their departure. Mary was always the practical daughter in that respect.

Kitty and Lydia's arguments filled the stairwell and Elizabeth took a deep breath before she and Jane climbed the stairs to the second floor of the house.

"You would think they hated each other," Jane whispered.

"Sometimes I do wonder," Elizabeth replied.

They knew very well that the two girls loved each other to distraction, but their constant arguments made such a thing seem impossible, especially to any outside eye.

Safe in their own bedchamber, Jane went to the wardrobe to remove her gowns for examination. She held a pale ivory gown to her shoulders and regarded her reflection in the looking glass thoughtfully. "How strange it would be if Lydia was correct," she mused. "What a strange thing it would be if our younger sisters were married and mistresses of their own households before you or I had even gained a suitor?"

"Ridiculous," Elizabeth laughed. "If Lydia manages to find

herself a good husband with her antics I shall eat a handful of flowers from the gardens at their wedding breakfast for all to see."

Jane laughed and laid the gown on her bed. It was plain, but Jane was beautiful enough to distract from whatever she might choose to wear. It would also look well with the pearls that she had chosen for her hair.

Elizabeth stepped into her pale pink dress and pulled the puffed sleeves up over her shoulders. She had re-stitched the hems with a dark rose colored ribbon, and had asked Jane to pin ribbon roses made of the same velvet into her dark hair.

"I think you should wear that one," Elizabeth said as she fussed with the bodice of the gown. "The blue ribbon at the neckline is the same color as your eyes, the last time you wore it everyone remarked upon it. It suits you very well."

Jane let out a strangled noise and sat down on the edge of her bed with another gown draped over her lap.

"Does it ever seem hopeless to you, Lizzy?" Jane asked suddenly.

Elizabeth looked at her sister carefully, unsure of how to answer.

It was true that she had begun to doubt that she would ever find the love she knew she deserved in Hertfordshire, but she had said anything to her sister, or mentioned any of her heavy thoughts and misgivings about such things. Their mother seemed undaunted by the lack of options to be found, but Elizabeth could not be coaxed into any excitement about her prospects.

"Why would you ask such a thing? Have you given up hope?" Elizabeth hoped that her reply did not give any indication of her own fears, but Jane seemed too distracted to notice as she plucked at the ribbons at the neckline of her gown.

Jane sighed heavily. "It has been difficult to find any sort of positivity on this subject. I know in my heart that I shall find my own happiness, and that I must be patient."

Elizabeth smiled. "We must both be patient and hope that we may have as much happiness as our other friends..."

Jane pulled her dress over her head and then grabbed her sister's hands and held them lightly. "We shall endeavor to have a wonderful evening."

Elizabeth's heart lifted just a little as she squeezed Jane's fingers. "We shall, indeed."

"I do not know why you insist that Mary should come at all," Lydia growled as Elizabeth once again retrieved her gloves from her youngest sister's hands and returned them to a pouting Kitty.

Mrs. Bennet waved her fan dismissively. "Mary may not enjoy such frivolities, but she is not old enough to decline."

"Not as yet," Mary said softly enough that her mother could not hear, but Elizabeth, who was standing nearby to help Kitty with her shawl, heard it clearly enough.

Poor Mary.

Society events such as the assemblies and seasonal balls were not her preferred form of entertainment. She preferred the infrequent salons that Lady Lucas hosted where she could play the pianoforte and indulge in conversation that she found worthy of her time, and where her compositions and concertos were more appreciated.

After many complaints, more arguments over who was wearing what, and assurances that the new officers who had just arrived in Meryton would, indeed, be present, the Bennet family in its entirety were finally able to clamber into the waiting carriage and depart for the assembly rooms. Mr. Bennet had done his best to avoid the evening, but his wife would not be deterred, and Elizabeth lost count of the amount of deep sighs that emanated from her father's direction as the carriage rolled toward town.

Conversation during their short journey was, as always, dominated by Lydia and Kitty, who competed needlessly for their mother's attention and approval while Jane and Elizabeth did their best to keep them otherwise occupied.

An exercise in futility, to be certain.

When the carriage finally lurched to a stop, Elizabeth was more than eager to leave the confines of her seat and breathe in the cool evening air.

Lydia and Kitty pushed past Elizabeth and Jane in their haste to run up the stairs and into the assembly rooms and Elizabeth glared after them. Shouting would do nothing, and it would only earn her a scolding from her mother.

She had Jane entered the ballroom together, but as soon as they stepped through the doors, Jane was immediately led away by Mrs. Bennet and her father detoured to the card room to meet the other gentlemen of his circle. Mary found a chair and sat down with a disgruntled look upon her face, while Lydia and Kitty's laughter could be heard from the dance floor. Thus abandoned, Elizabeth went in search of Charlotte Lucas.

Her friend stood at the edge of the assembly hall and held a glass of untouched rum punch in one gloved hand. She looked decidedly uninterested in everything that was happening, but as soon as she met Elizabeth's eyes, her mood brightened immediately.

"Lizzy! I am so very pleased to see you," she greeted her warmly. "Mama was not certain that you would be coming—"

"There will never be any assembly, ball, dinner party, or country dance that Lydia and Kitty would allow us to ignore," Elizabeth said with a smile. "You know as well as I that I had no choice in the matter."

"I can see them now," Charlotte laughed. "Always eager to dance."

"Always eager to be the center of attention," Elizabeth agreed ruefully.

"I have been so looking forward to your arrival," Charlotte murmured and Elizabeth felt a smile creep across her face. Though she pretended not to be, Charlotte Lucas was very much like her mother, and Lady Lucas was very fond of gossip.

Thanks to her father's title and her mother's proclivity for such conversations, Charlotte was uniquely positioned in Meryton's society to hear many things that Elizabeth would not otherwise be privy to.

Elizabeth helped herself to a glass of punch from one of the many trays that were being passed through the room. On the dance floor, Lydia and Kitty were already hanging upon the arms of two handsome young officers that she did not recognize, and, as usual, Mrs. Bennet was deeply embroiled in some discussion or other with her circle of friends.

Poor Jane stood to the side of their mother's conversation, hoping to be released but knowing that she could not leave until someone asked her to dance or she was dismissed.

Elizabeth frowned slightly and then focused on her friend. "Come now, I have been too long without any news, pray do not keep me in suspense any longer."

This was what Charlotte wanted to hear, of course, and Elizabeth could not help but feel a trifle guilty for excluding Jane from this gossip. She would have to remember every detail to recount to her sister once they had returned to Longbourn.

"There is talk in Meryton is simply too good to keep to myself," Charlotte replied with a secretive smile. "As you must be aware by now, Papa went to visit Mr. Bingley some weeks ago," she began.

Elizabeth's eyebrow rose slightly. Of course, her mother had talked of nothing else as Mr. Bennet had, as yet, not visited Netherfield Park... or, if he had, he had said nothing of it.

"As you have also presumably heard, Mr. Bingley is exceedingly gentlemanlike, and has a pleasant enough countenance. He arrived at the assembly with his sisters and two other gentlemen not long before you did, Lizzy. From what I have observed, he has a very unaffected manner to him, and is very quick to smile... A trait not often found in gentlemen of his station."

"Really, Charlotte," Elizabeth laughed. "Are all gentlemen in possession of good fortunes joyless creatures with no cause to smile?"

"I would not know," Charlotte replied and then laughed lightly. "But it may very well explain the frown upon the face of the gentleman who accompanied him."

"How very dull, indeed," Elizabeth said. "Give me a poor man who laughs too much over a dour rich man with no good humor to speak of."

"Indeed," Charlotte replied and Elizabeth could not determine whether her friend truly agreed with her. But it was impossible to assume anything when it came to Charlotte's unspoken thoughts.

"But then there are Mr. Bingley's sisters," Charlotte said. She lifted her glass of punch in the vague direction of two women who looked entirely out of place in their fine gowns and dyed ostrich plumes amid the whirl of country finery. "Miss Bingley and Mrs. Hurst... they are very refined women, decidedly more interested in fashion than one might expect for a place like Meryton. I can only assume that they were expecting London society as opposed to our own..."

Elizabeth narrowed her eyes at her friend. This was most unlike her. "Charlotte, you are keeping something from me," Elizabeth said teasingly.

Charlotte smiled and her cheeks flushed slightly. "I am, indeed. But there is more discussion swirling through Meryton about the gentleman who accompanied Mr. Bingley this evening.

"Which one?" Elizabeth asked. She tilted her chin vaguely at Mr. Bingley's sisters once more. "The one standing near Mrs. Hurst could only be her husband. A woman who looks as self-important as she could only have a husband with his nose always in a drink."

Elizabeth was only speaking as she observed, for the gentleman standing nearest to Mrs. Hurst had already quaffed two glasses of red wine in the short amount of time that she had been watching him.

"Dreadful," she muttered.

"No, no. That is Mr. Hurst. Husband to Mr. Bingley's eldest sister."

"I am grateful to hear it," Elizabeth said with a dramatic sigh.

"It is the *other* gentleman that I speak of now, Lizzy. The one with the dour countenance. He is rumored to be a great friend of Mr. Bingley's... And my mother has also learned that he is in possession of a great estate and has an income of more than ten thousand a year... Why, some of the ladies have even said that he is handsomer than Mr. Bingley."

"A good income can be a remarkable aphrodisiac," Elizabeth murmured as she scanned the crowd for unfamiliar faces.

"Mr. Bingley has done very well to make himself acquainted with all the principal people in the room," Charlotte continued. "He has been very agreeable and danced every dance, and has even talked of giving a ball of his own at Netherfield Park when Christmas approaches."

Elizabeth laughed shortly and took a sip of her punch. The taste of rum was very strong, and she resolved to only have a few glasses, and very sparingly. She did not like to feel out of control—especially in a setting such as this when many eyes were upon her. "He has been in town only a short while and is already planning his own society functions," Elizabeth mused. "How very bold, indeed. But perhaps it is a *welcome* sort of boldness."

Elizabeth craned her neck and noticed with a thrill that she had located the mysterious Mr. Bingley. He was fair, and handsome in his own way; but his looks were not to Elizabeth's taste.

A dark haired gentleman with a wild mane of dark hair that curled over his collar stood near Mr. Bingley. But while the first gentleman engaged in lively conversation with a gentleman that Elizabeth recognized as the father of another young woman of a similar age and social station to herself—Mr. Everley was enamored of the sound of his own voice, at least that was her father's impression of him.

The mysterious stranger with Mr. Bingley stood apart from the conversation, and did not seem to be listening at all. He was tall, taller than his friend, and his jacket was finely tailored and made of what was surely an expensive material that Elizabeth longed to run her fingertips over.

He was certainly *very* handsome.

"And what of his friend?" Elizabeth asked suddenly.

Charlotte raised an eyebrow and shook her head. "His friend... Well, Lizzy, I can only tell you what I have observed.

Wherever Mr. Bingley goes, Mr. Darcy is certain to follow. Mr. Darcy will invite one young lady to dance and Mr. Darcy will immediately invite another. He does not appear to be as gregarious or generous with his smiles as Mr. Bingley, but he is *very* handsome... And if the young ladies are to be believed, he is quite an accomplished dancer."

"You are a wealth of information this evening," Elizabeth said dryly. Charlotte flushed a darker shade of pink, but did not make any attempt to deny Elizabeth's assessment.

"One does one's best to stay informed of such things," she said as she sipped at her punch.

"Indeed." Elizabeth looked around the room once more and sighed heavily. "No matter how many young officers come to join the garrison, there are still entirely too many ladies in attendance and not enough partners." She frowned slightly as Lydia's laughter echoed above the music. "It does not help matters that my own sisters will not take their turn without a partner."

Jane had finally broken away from their mother and was beginning to move toward the dance floor, and Elizabeth immediately felt a pang of guilt. Here she was, gossiping with Charlotte while the rest of her sisters enjoyed the assembly in their own ways.

Elizabeth had come to dance and reconnect with her friends, and as much as she loved Charlotte, she had not planned to stand in one place all evening.

Unfortunately, when she apologized to Charlotte and left her side, Elizabeth had been obliged, by the scarcity of gentlemen that she had just complained about, to sit down for two dances. During her quiet moments while watching the dancing, Elizabeth pondered Charlotte's words. Jane had accepted an invitation to dance from a slender young man who seemed uncomfortable in his officer's jacket, but Elizabeth could see that her sister's eyes returned often to the fair-haired gentleman who stood nearby.

While Elizabeth waited for a lull in the dancing, she had been positioned in such a way as to overhear a conversation between Mr. Bingley and his friend.

"Come now," said Mr. Bingley, "you can see for yourself, she is the handsomest woman in the room. I must have a dance with her."

The other man shook his head. "She is uncommonly pretty, I grant you, but have you determined who she has come with?" he asked. "I refuse to be obliged to dance with a partner with all the grace of a market pony."

Elizabeth lifted a hand to her mouth to hide her smile. She knew she should not have been listening, but she could not prevent it. It was very rare that she could overhear gentlemen speaking to each other when they believed no one else was listening.

"I would not be so fastidious as you are," said Mr. Bingley, "Not for a kingdom! Upon my honour, I never met with so many pleasant girls in my life as I have this evening; and there are several of them that are very pretty, indeed."

"You, my friend, are intent on dancing with the only handsome girl in the room," said the other gentleman dryly. "We are, indeed, in the heart of the country."

Elizabeth glanced over at the pair and saw a genuine smile break over Mr. Bingley's handsome face. "Truly! She is the most beautiful creature I ever beheld! But there is one of her sisters sitting down just behind you, who is very pretty, and I dare say very agreeable."

Elizabeth looked away quickly and felt a hot blush flood her cheeks. They were speaking of her now... This could not end in anything but disaster...

"Which do you mean?" said the gentleman.

Without meaning to, Elizabeth dared to glance back at the pair, and in doing so caught the tall gentleman's eye for only a moment before she looked away.

The dance ended and Jane rushed over to her. "Lizzy, you have been sitting so close to Mr. Bingley this entire time—tell me, what do you think of him? Could you hear his conversation?" Jane's voice was low and breathless and Elizabeth smiled at her sister's eagerness.

"Charlotte tells me that he has danced with nearly every young lady in the room," she said. "And that in addition to being very handsome, he is also a very agreeable sort of gentleman. Of course, this could all be lies—"

Jane smacked her sister lightly with her fan. "Do not be horrid," she scolded in a teasing tone. All at once, Jane's jovial expression faded from her face and Elizabeth turned in her chair to see what she was looking at. "Lizzy... Oh, Lizzy, he is coming this way. Is that other gentleman his friend?"

"Yes," Elizabeth whispered. "Mr. Darcy. Charlotte said that he has a very fine estate, but I would say that he needs to smile more often."

"Pardon me," Mr. Bingley said as he came upon them. Jane stood up from her seat in a rush and hauled her sister up with her. "I thought I would enquire as to the state of your dance card."

He was speaking to Jane, but Elizabeth took the opportunity to speak first as she drew Jane's card from her reticule and examined it closely.

She pretended to ponder its contents very seriously before she smiled. "I daresay that my sister is available for the next three or four dances," she said brightly. "Perhaps even five, but there might be some gossip you were to take every available dance for yourself..."

A smile broke over Mr. Bingley's face as Jane blushed furiously and snatched her dance card from Elizabeth's hand.

"Ah! Mr. Bingley!" Sir William's familiar shout echoed in Elizabeth's ears and she forced herself to smile as the portly older gentleman inserted himself into the conversation.

"Mr. Bingley you have had the very distinct pleasure to meet Miss Jane Bennet and Miss Elizabeth Bennet of Longbourn. Their father is very highly regarded in Meryton, why just the other week I heard from one of my dear friends—"

"Miss Bennet," Mr. Bingley said, bowing low. "And Miss Bennet. I am, that is to say, *we* are delighted to meet you both."

Elizabeth and Jane performed their dutiful curtsies while the gentlemen bowed, and Elizabeth felt a flush of her own creep up her neck as she caught Mr. Darcy's dark gaze. He did not smile, but his eyes were full of an emotion that Elizabeth could not identify.

Unbothered by Mr. Bingley's interruption, Sir William continued with his boisterous introductions. "Miss Jane, Miss Elizabeth, might I present Mr. Charles Bingley, lately of London, and now of Netherfield Park, and Mr. Fitzwilliam Darcy, of Derbyshire who has very kindly deigned to come to Hertfordshire for a little change of pace."

Mr. Bingley nodded somewhat awkwardly to Sir William, and then stepped closer to Jane and favored her with a charming smile. "Are you fond of dancing, Miss Bennet?" he asked and gave his friend a meaningful glance.

"Oh, indeed," Jane replied happily.

"And you, Miss Elizabeth?" Mr. Darcy asked suddenly.

"I do, when there are enough partners to be had," she replied airily.

Behind them, the musicians played the final notes of the dance and those on the floor bowed to their partners and began to take new positions.

"Then I daresay this is the perfect moment," Mr. Bingley said with a brilliant smile. He extended his elbow to Jane, who took it eagerly, but then turned to her sister.

"Lizzy, will you be quite alright if I—"

"Miss Elizabeth Bennet," Mr. Darcy said, "if you would do me the honor?" He stepped and offered Elizabeth his arm.

"Quite well," Elizabeth said to her sister with a smile as she set her hand upon Mr. Darcy's proffered elbow. Jane fairly floated across the floor on Mr. Bingley's arm and Elizabeth found herself surprisingly happy to see them together. Perhaps it would not be so bold to hope that Jane's melancholy could be eclipsed by the attentions of a handsome gentleman. He had already spoken highly of her without even speaking with her—and Jane was an accomplished and intelligent young woman. It would be no surprise to Elizabeth if the gentleman was half in love with her sister by the time the dance ended.

As they moved toward the dance floor, Elizabeth could also not escape noticing the look upon their mother's face as they passed by.

"Do you see, Mrs. Hartford! My girls upon the arms of the wealthiest bachelors in the room! So much for your officers..." Mrs. Bennet exclaimed. Elizabeth cringed as her mother waved her fan in their direction and she hoped that the gentlemen had not overheard her brash words.

She glanced over at Mr. Darcy, but he seemed not to have heard anything, and Mr. Bingley was engaged in conversation with Jane and thusly distracted from any offence that might have been taken.

As they took their positions, Elizabeth did her best to ignore the stares and whispers of her friends and neighbors. They would have all, by now, heard the news of Mr. Darcy's income... But to see that the wealthiest gentlemen in the room had chosen the two eldest Bennet girls to pay their attentions to? Most uncommon, indeed.

She could not see her mother, but from her initial reaction, Elizabeth could only assume that Mrs. Bennet would call this moment one of her proudest.

"I did not expect to meet someone like you in Hertfordshire," Mr. Darcy said as the dance began.

"Whatever do you mean," Elizabeth asked. "I believe I am the same as any other young woman in Meryton."

"Oh, I think not," the gentleman said thoughtfully. "You are very interesting, indeed… In possession of fine eyes, a quick wit… I am certain there are other qualities that require admiration."

Elizabeth laughed lightly and chose to ignore the flare of pleasure in her chest at his compliments. She had heard the flattery of many officers and gentlemen at the Meryton assemblies, but all of their praise had felt hollow in comparison to Mr. Darcy's words and her cheeks flushed with warmth.

"You are too kind, Mr. Darcy," she said demurely.

He shook his head and took her hand for another step in the dance and Elizabeth was grateful for her gloves so that he could not feel how warm her skin had suddenly become. "Gossip must sweep through Meryton at an alarming speed." His dark chuckle sent a jolt through her spine and she knew that he had heard her sharp intake of breath at the sound.

"Gossip?"

Elizabeth looked away and tried to focus on her steps, but she could feel the gentleman's dark eyes watching her every movement.

"Indeed. The arrival of two new gentlemen in Hertfordshire must be a very popular topic of conversation."

"Oh, yes, of course," Elizabeth replied. "But I confess that I have not heard any…"

It was a lie, of course, but she did not know what she should say. Of course there had been gossip, but the gentleman who was now her dancing partner did not match the descriptions that she had been given of him. He was tall and broad-shouldered, and she liked the way his eyes glinted when he smiled.

All at once, Elizabeth realized that she had been staring at him. She looked out into the crowd of people in the assembly hall, desperate to look anywhere but into the smoldering eyes of the gentleman she danced with. She caught her mother's eye as they spun past and Elizabeth groaned inwardly at the sight of her.

From the smile upon Mrs. Bennet's face, it was clear that she knew *precisely* how much income Elizabeth's dancing partner had to his name and quite possibly the name of his estate, as well.

"And your sister," Mr. Darcy said suddenly, "is she entertaining any suitors at the moment?"

Elizabeth looked at him in surprise. "Jane? No, indeed." She glanced over at her sister and Mr. Bingley and noted the smile upon Jane's face. Her heart lifted to see Jane so happy, and she hoped that something would come of this evening—even if it was only another dance. It may have been strange to hope that there would be more to come from something as simple as a dance, but there was no way to be certain.

"And you, Miss Elizabeth? Are *you* entertaining any suitors?" Mr. Darcy asked.

The question surprised her, and she looked up into his eyes incredulously. "Me? Oh—"

The final bars of the dance sounded and she curtseyed to her partner as she was meant to, but Mr. Darcy's grip upon her hand lingered for a few beats longer than it should have.

Elizabeth bit her lip briefly and then smiled at him without answering.

Mr. Bingley tapped Mr. Darcy on the shoulder, and the gentleman turned briefly to speak to his friend.

An officer standing nearby took advantage of Mr. Darcy's distraction and bowed as he took his place across from Elizabeth. She looked over her shoulder at her mother who was gesturing desperately for her to partner with Mr. Darcy once more, but she did not have a chance.

The musicians launched into the next piece of music, and Elizabeth smiled at the exuberant officer and took the hand he offered her. The officer was bright and cheerful, and newly arrived in Hertfordshire from a village near the seaside that Elizabeth had not heard of before. But no matter how hard she tried to focus on what the young man was saying, Elizabeth could not ignore the fact that Mr. Fitzwilliam Darcy was standing at the edge of the dance floor staring at her. She could feel his scrutiny, and every time her partner turned her, her eyes met the dark intensity of Mr. Darcy's gaze and it made her heart beat faster to see the small smile upon his lips as he watched her dance with the lanky officer who had usurped his position.

When the dance ended, Mr. Darcy was there at her elbow before Elizabeth could turn away to give another young lady the opportunity to dance.

"But Mr. Darcy, there are not enough gentlemen... It would be impolite of me—"

"Then we shall be impolite," he said with a smile as he took her hand to begin the next dance.

Elizabeth's cheeks burned as she performed the first steps of the dance. To her left, Jane was still partnered with Mr. Bingley, and seemed to be entirely oblivious to the fact that there were other young ladies waiting their turn to dance. It was entirely unlike her sister to be so selfish, and entirely improper to dance with the same partner for more than two dances in a row... But if Jane could forget such things, so could she.

She smiled at Mr. Darcy and continued the dance, with such a handsome and agreeable partner at her side, no one could argue with her desire to stay upon the floor.

For dance after dance, Elizabeth ignored her mother's desperate gestures and anguished expressions and enjoyed the attentions of her partner. It had been many years since she had spent so much time dancing at an assembly, but she did not notice the passage of time.

Mr. Darcy asked about her family, about her home, and about her life in Hertfordshire. No gentleman had ever shown such an interest in her, and Elizabeth was charmed beyond measure.

In a break between dances, Elizabeth and Mr. Darcy stood to the side of the room while Elizabeth tried her best to cool her cheeks and regain control of her pounding heart.

"Had I known that Hertfordshire was such a delightful place populated with such delightful society, I should have begged Charles to come here all the earlier," he said as he handed her a glass of punch which Elizabeth drank gratefully.

"I daresay such things are very difficult to predict," Elizabeth said after a moment. "The society changes from month to month on account of the garrison, and those of us who reside here in a more permanent manner are more like shrubbery in the garden of Meryton's society..."

"Shrubbery?" Mr. Darcy laughed.

"Indeed," Elizabeth said. She gestured toward the officers in their bright red regimental jackets. "In the autumn, the flowers bloom, and then they are gone come summer when the garrison moves to Brighton... when they return for Christmas, all changes again. Red berries against winter snows."

Elizabeth paused briefly, hoping that she had not spoken too strangely for Mr. Darcy's liking, but he seemed to find her more amusing than strange and Elizabeth was heartened by his smile and the way his eyes glinted in the candlelight.

"You are a very interesting young woman, Miss Elizabeth Bennet," he said thoughtfully.

"One does what one can with what is given," Elizabeth said simply. She pointed to the dance floor where Jane and Mr. Bingley whirled through another dance. "Your friend seems to be quite enjoying the assembly."

Mr. Darcy smiled, though Elizabeth noted how briefly the expression lingered on his handsome face. "Indeed," he looked back at her and Elizabeth felt a pleasant shiver as his eyes met hers. "And you? Is this evening everything you hoped it would be, Miss Bennet?"

Elizabeth blinked at him in surprise as she realized that she had not expected much from the assembly at all... She had known that there would be precious few opportunities to dance, and that she would have to limit herself when it came to punch —but here she was, drinking her third glass of very strong punch and talking to a gentleman who was worth over ten thousand pounds a year. A very unexpected outcome, indeed.

"It is not..." Elizabeth managed to say.

"In a good way?" he asked.

Elizabeth nodded, sipped at her punch, and dragged her eyes away from the intensity of the gentleman's gaze. "Indeed," she replied.

·　·　·

The remaining hours of the assembly passed more quickly than Elizabeth had expected. Mr. Darcy left her side for only two dances to partner with Mr. Bingley's sisters, and Mr. Bingley never once stepped too far away from Jane to be pulled into another dance with any other partner.

It was obvious to Elizabeth that her sister was quite taken with the gentleman from London, and she could not blame her. By the time the guests began to leave the assembly rooms, Elizabeth began to feel as though she herself were on her way to developing some affection for Mr. Darcy, as well.

It was Lydia who pulled her away from the gentleman's company and begged her to come to the carriage.

"Lizzy, I am exhausted," she whined. "And my feet ache." Elizabeth blinked at her youngest sister in surprise for it was usually Lydia who had to be pried away from the dance floor or from the arm of a particularly roguish looking officer.

"You must excuse me," Elizabeth said to Mr. Darcy with some embarrassment. "I did not realize how late—"

"No apologies are required for an evening well spent," he said with a smile. He bowed low and Elizabeth's cheeks warmed with pleasure to have him smile at her in such a way. She had been right to believe that he should smile more often. But if the heat in her cheeks were any indication, perhaps it would be better for her if he did not smile...

Mr. Bingley bowed similarly to Jane as Kitty pulled her elder sister away toward the ballroom doors.

"Mama is *waiting*," Lydia hissed.

"Yes. Yes, of course," Elizabeth said. She walked away from the gentleman reluctantly and Jane and Kitty met them at the doors.

Charlotte Lucas tried to waylay her and laid a hand upon Elizabeth's arm as she passed. "Lizzy," she said quietly. "I was astonished to see you stand up with Mr. Darcy, you must tell me about him…"

"Perhaps later, Charlotte," Elizabeth sighed. *Much later.*

Charlotte would have to wait for her gossip. Elizabeth had enough to think about, and she had to talk to Jane about what had happened that evening. No doubt her sister would have much to say about Mr. Charles Bingley, and Elizabeth was eager to hear all of it.

2
————

The return to Longbourn passed in a blur that Elizabeth barely remembered except for the fact that their mother would not cease in her exclamations of joy in regards to the events she had witnessed upon the dance floor. Indeed, much to the chagrin of their younger sisters, it was all Mrs. Bennet wanted to talk about.

Mr. Bennet had departed the assembly with Mary some hours before, but that was a normal occurrence. Mary was always all too eager to leave, especially as soon as their mother turned her attention to Jane and Elizabeth's good fortune.

Their arrival at Longbourn was a relief, and Elizabeth fairly jumped from the carriage in an effort to escape their mother's endless plans for their inevitable double wedding, which would, of course, be hosted at Netherfield Park.

Jane exited the carriage with a look of strained relief on her face. She looped her arm through Elizabeth's as they walked across the courtyard to the house. Kitty and Lydia dragged their feet and whined about how exhausted they were after the exertions of the assembly, which was entirely unlike their usual behavior after a dance...

Typically, Lydia would carry on loudly about how many more officers she had danced with than Kitty had, and then Kitty would argue that it was untrue—it had always been so. But that evening was different, and Elizabeth was taken by surprise. Perhaps it was that all of their mother's attention had been focused upon Jane and Elizabeth in equal measure, and not upon her younger daughters and their teasing frivolities.

In the past, Elizabeth had gone up to bed grateful not to be the one under her mother's scrutiny, but Mr. Darcy's attentions had changed all of that.

Thankfully, Mrs. Bennet was distracted by her eagerness to tell her dear husband of what had transpired after his departure from the assembly and did not waylay her daughters for too long. The hour was very late, and there would be time enough to discuss every moment of the assembly over breakfast the next morning.

Kitty and Lydia marched up the stairs to their bedchamber without so much as a whine to stay up for a glass of the mulled wine that Mrs. Hill had just begun making in preparation for the approaching cold weather. A pot was always simmering on the stove

"Oh, Mr. Bennet!" their mother cried as she flounced down the corridor toward her husband's study. "You shall *never* believe what has happened—"

"We must go up to bed now, Lizzy," Jane said in a hushed tone, "if we do not, Mama will call for us to come into Papa's study and confirm all of her stories."

Elizabeth covered her mouth to smother her laughter and nodded. "I do believe you are correct," she said.

They rushed up the stairs and laughed quietly together as they did so.

"Do, please, keep your voices down," Kitty demanded from

the doorway of the bedchamber she shared with Lydia. "We are *very* tired."

Elizabeth's eyes widened at this reversal of the scolding that was typically delivered by herself or Jane on any other evening. After any dance or dinner party, she and Jane would lie awake for hours listening to their younger sisters as they laughed and talked into the early morning hours.

Jane apologized softly and she and Elizabeth fled into their bedchamber and did not collapse into giggles until the door was closed behind them.

"Oh, Lizzy," Jane said breathlessly as she leaned against the door, "what a wonderful evening."

Elizabeth fell into the chair at the vanity and began to unpin her hair as Jane twirled about the room and then collapsed upon her bed.

"He was the most wonderful dancer," Jane sighed and then she sat up suddenly. "And *you*, my dear Lizzy... You danced with the wealthiest gentleman in the room, and barely flinched! Any other young lady would have been a nervous wreck to be upon his arm! Mama said there were several jealous faces in the crowd..."

"I confess that I did not notice," Elizabeth said with a hint of chagrin. "I had not expected to be so—"

"Distracted?"

"Indeed," Elizabeth laughed.

"And what do you think of my dear Charles Bingley?" Jane asked.

Elizabeth turned in her chair and leaned upon the back to look at her sister's smiling face. Jane was positively glowing with happiness and Elizabeth's heart felt lighter than it ever had before as she beheld her sister's joy.

"He was very handsome, in his own way," she said.

"In his own way?" Jane said incredulously. "I daresay he is the handsomest gentleman I ever beheld!"

Elizabeth laughed and shook her head at the similarity of her sister's words to the declaration that Mr. Bingley's had made. "As you say," she said. "But aside from that, he was every inch a gentleman, and you danced together very well. I was very impressed to see a gentleman from London performing the steps of a country dance with such confidence."

Jane's smile was brilliant and happy. "He was, indeed, very comfortable upon the dance floor. I cannot recall the last time I danced so much at an assembly!"

Elizabeth turned back to the mirror and plucked the velvet ribbon roses from her hair. She smiled at her sister's reflection. "I have been struggling to remember the very same thing," she said.

"And what of your gentleman, Lizzy?" Jane asked as Elizabeth rose from the chair to give her sister the opportunity to unpin her own hair.

"He was *very* handsome," Elizabeth said. "And asked me a good many questions—more than any other gentleman I have spoken with."

"Questions?"

"About Longbourn. The garrison. The former occupants of Netherfield Park... other things."

"Other things?" Jane laughed.

"Yes," Elizabeth replied with a smile. Jane did not need to know *everything*. "Now Mr. Bingley—did he ask *you* any questions?"

"Of course," Jane replied. "He was very curious about our family, and the name of Papa's lawyer..."

"Papa's lawyer?"

"Yes, he wanted to engage someone here in Meryton to see to his business affairs."

"So, he plans to stay at Netherfield Park for some time, then?" Elizabeth asked as she untied the ribbons at the shoulder of her gown and stepped out of it.

"It would seem so," Jane replied. "Oh, but Lizzy, what do you *think* of him?"

Elizabeth considered her sister's hopeful face for a moment and then pulled her nightgown from her wardrobe.

"You are an excellent judge of character, Jane. If *you* believe that this gentleman is sincere in his interest, then I can see no reason for you to feel any unease... I certainly have no complaint to level in his direction. I believe that you may fairly judge a man by his friends, and while I confess I initially held some concern for his... demeanor... Mr. Darcy has proven himself to be as pleasant as Mr. Bingley."

Jane's delighted smile was the only encouragement Elizabeth needed. She bent to kiss her sister's pink cheek and then turned down the lamp and climbed beneath her coverlet.

"I do believe it," Jane sighed as she unwound the ribbon that held her golden curls in place. "Perhaps we might find our happiness after all, Lizzy, and I had begun to give up hope that it would ever be possible."

Elizabeth did not say that she agreed, but it was difficult to deny that she had entertained the same dark thoughts. She had never been given to despair, but Elizabeth had noticed that her sister's happy demeanor had faded in the last year.

She blew out her candle and settled back against her pillows as Jane turned down the remaining lamps and slid beneath the blankets of her own bed.

"Perhaps tomorrow we can walk into Meryton," Jane said through a yawn.

"Perhaps," Elizabeth agreed. Her eyelids were heavy, and before Jane had blown out her own candle, Elizabeth was asleep.

3

———

A full week went by before Mrs. Bennet was able to talk of something more than the events of the assembly. They had all waited with baited breath for any word to come from Netherfield Park, but there had been nothing, and Jane's happiness began to fade somewhat.

However, preparations had already begun for the next social event, and Kitty and Lydia begged endlessly to be allowed to walk into Meryton to look at the ribbons in Mrs. Addison's shop. In need of some distraction, Jane made the request on their behalf, and Mr. Bennet was happy to grant it if only to gain some peace and quiet in the house.

That morning, Elizabeth elected to stay behind while her Jane and the younger girls walked into town. Their mother would likely stay abed for a large enough portion of the day that Elizabeth knew she would be able to read, undisturbed and uninterrupted, in a quiet house while Mary worked on her sheet music and her father was shut away in his study.

Elizabeth waved a dutiful farewell to her sisters as Kitty and Lydia ran ahead through the courtyard with Jane walking quickly behind them to keep up.

She closed the front door and went to the parlor to settle herself with a book that she had been neglecting for far longer than she cared to admit. The faint sound of Mary practicing her scales at the pianoforte floated down the corridor pleasantly enough, and Elizabeth sighed contentedly as she settled into a chair and opened her book.

Moments like these were rare in the Bennet household, and Elizabeth had no intention of wasting this opportunity for solace.

However, she had only just opened her book when Mrs. Hill appeared at the parlor door. The housekeeper's expression could only be described as one of hopeful curiosity and Elizabeth set her book down with some trepidation.

"What is it?" she asked.

The housekeeper smiled warmly. "Well, Miss Lizzy, there is a gentleman at the door. Two gentlemen, in fact. Officers by the look of them, from the garrison. Perhaps they have been sent by Colonel Forster..."

Mrs. Hill's words were rushed and full of barely contained excitement. It was not often that any gentlemen of note visited Longbourn. And if any gentlemen *did* happen to approach the house, they were usually married, or family.

Elizabeth set down her book and rose from her chair with as much calmness as she could manage. "Are they here to see Papa?" she asked.

Mrs. Hill shook her head.

Of course, not, if they had been, the housekeeper would have taken them to his study directly instead of coming to her.

"They asked to see Miss Lydia," she replied.

"Lydia?" Elizabeth frowned briefly. *What kind of an impression had Lydia made on these officers?*

"I will speak to them," Elizabeth said with a sigh.

Mrs. Hill nodded excitedly and bustled down the corridor

toward the foyer. Elizabeth could hear her telling the waiting men that she was on her way, and she steeled herself for whatever trouble Lydia had managed to make for herself.

Mrs. Hill stood by the stairs as Elizabeth came to the door and the gentlemen bowed at the waist as they greeted her.

Elizabeth brightened immediately to see the familiar face of one of Lydia's favorite officers.

"Why, Mr. Denny, I did not think to see you here this morning," she said.

The officer in question was a stocky young man with hay-colored hair and a pleasant, if boyish, face. He smiled broadly and Elizabeth was coerced into a smile herself by his familiarly jovial reaction to seeing her.

"Miss Elizabeth Bennet, I am very pleased to see you this fine morning! We came with the intent to ask if Miss Lydia and Miss Catherine would be available to walk with us—"

Elizabeth turned her attention to the gentleman standing beside Mr. Denny and blinked in surprise to see an unfamiliar face instead of the one she had expected.

Mr. Denny noted her curiosity and made haste to introduce his fellow officer. "Ah, yes, this is Mr. Wickham, he has newly arrived at the garrison from—where is it that you are from again, man? I scarcely remember!"

"Newtown, Miss Bennet," the taller man said mildly as he bowed slightly at the waist.

"Yes, of course," Mr. Denny laughed. "There are so many new officers in Meryton that I confess that I am having trouble keeping my facts correct."

This Mr. Wickham was a welcome sight, indeed. Tall and lithely built, with broad shoulders and a darkly handsome face, Elizabeth suspected that he was quite a few years older than the bright and enthusiastic Mr. Denny. He seemed a quiet sort, and

Elizabeth could not help but notice the gentleman's quiet appraisal of her.

"You are most welcome to Hertfordshire, Mr. Wickham," she said quickly. "It is a pity that you have missed the assembly, it would have been a perfect opportunity to become acquainted with your new neighbors."

"New friends, I should hope," Mr. Wickham said. "Indeed, I was too late in arriving to attend the assembly, but I have heard that it was a very enjoyable evening, indeed."

"Splendid," Mr. Denny agreed enthusiastically. "You did miss a most excellent evening."

"If the dancing partners are half as beautiful as you have said, then I am very regretful, indeed," Mr. Wickham said with a smile that was directed at Elizabeth. She shifted slightly on her feet and tried to ignore the warmth in her cheeks and focus on the reason for the officers' visit.

She lifted her chin and straightened her shoulders so as not to betray her sudden nervousness. "I am sorry to say, Mr. Denny, that my sisters have gone into Meryton for the afternoon," she said hurriedly. "But I shall tell her that you called. Lydia will be miserable to know that she has missed you, and the opportunity to meet your friend."

"I thank you, Miss Elizabeth," Mr. Denny said and executed a sweeping bow. "We shall go into Meryton, and hope for the joy of seeing your sisters there."

"Indeed," Elizabeth replied.

The officers made their departure after more bowing and wished her a good day several times before they turned and walked away through the courtyard and toward the road. Mr. Wickham, for his part, looked over his shoulder at her no less than three times, and each time Elizabeth felt her chest tighten just a very little. He was, indeed, very handsome, and more to her taste in height and temperament than a gentleman such as Mr. Denny.

When she finally pulled herself away from the door and closed it, she avoided Mrs. Hill's questioning looks. She had no desire to gossip with the housekeeper as the younger girls or their mother might do—it would be enough that Mrs. Hill would take the news of the officers' visit to her mistress. Elizabeth knew that it would only be a matter of time before she would have to answer more questions about it than she wanted to.

Elizabeth returned to the parlor and settled into her chair once more, but no matter how she tried to concentrate on the words upon the page, she could not stop thinking about Mr. Wickham and the way he had smiled at her.

What sort of a gentleman might he be?

Could he be compared to Mr. Darcy?

As the opportunity had never presented itself before, Elizabeth found herself wondering if a young lady might have two suitors. And, more importantly, what could be done about such a situation...

It was ridiculous to even consider such a thing.

As Elizabeth had predicted, Mr. Denny and Mr. Wickham's visit did not remain a secret for long. Upon her sisters' return to Longbourn, Mrs. Hill saw fit to reveal that the gentleman had come calling, and Elizabeth was immediately inundated with questions.

She could answer most of them easily enough, but Lydia's desperation for every tiny detail, down to the cut of the jackets the men had worn, brought Elizabeth to the very edge of her patience.

It did not help matters that she had to repeat every answer to similar questions posed by their mother who had deigned to come down from her chambers for supper. Mr. Bennet took supper in his study, and for the hundredth time Elizabeth envied him for his uncanny ability to escape the dining room whenever he pleased. Such absences usually coincided with changes in their mother's mood, and the few days leading up to, and following, any major social event. He would return to the table in good spirits after the excitement in the house had subsided, and Elizabeth often wished that she could do the same.

Nine days after the assembly, and two since Mr. Wickham's introduction, a letter arrived for Jane from Netherfield Park.

"Oh, Lizzy, it is an invitation to take tea with Miss Caroline Bingley and her sister, Mrs. Hurst at Netherfield Park!"

Elizabeth raised an eyebrow at her sister's enthusiasm for such a simple invitation, but it did not take long for her to discern the root of her sister's eagerness as Mrs. Bennet fairly leapt upon her daughter and pulled the invitation out of her hands.

"A very proper invitation, indeed," Mrs. Bennet exclaimed. "Look how refined her handwriting is... You would do well to cultivate friendships with these ladies, Jane—even *you* might learn something, Lizzy."

"Mama, surely—" Jane began, but Mrs. Bennet waved the invitation to silence her.

"If you are able to secure the affections of the sisters, it will be no trouble for them to speak well of you to their brother. Think of it, Jane, advocates for your happiness from within Netherfield Park, itself!"

Jane's cheeks flushed crimson and Elizabeth sighed heavily. There would be no distracting their mother from this course, she would have to console Jane privately about such embarrassment.

"In two days' time!" Mrs. Bennet said happily. "You have just enough warning to go into Meryton and purchase some new ribbons... You and Lizzy can go this afternoon!" She looked meaningfully at Elizabeth, who had just opened her mouth to protest such a command. "I will hear *no* arguments!"

Resigned to her mothers' direction, Jane pulled Elizabeth out of the room and they walked up to their bedchamber together to prepare for their walk into town. "I do not even know how I should dress," Jane said softly. "Miss Bingley and Mrs. Hurst are so very stylish, I fear that everything in my wardrobe will be woefully out of date in comparison."

"It should not matter in the slightest," Elizabeth said. "Miss Bingley and Mrs. Hurst should know that they cannot expect the height of London fashion to be on display here in Hertfordshire. One cannot expect us to dress our hair with pearls and ostrich feathers every day."

"This is very true... But why the invitation?" Jane mused.

"Can you not see?" Elizabeth laughed. "This is very certainly Mr. Bingley's doing. He could not invite you himself!"

A surprised expression crossed her sister's face and Elizabeth smiled as Jane exclaimed in a hushed tone, "you cannot be serious."

"Oh, but I am!"

They climbed the stairs in silence, but Elizabeth could see that her sister was considering her words carefully as they walked into the bedchamber they shared.

Jane opened the wardrobe as Elizabeth pulled out her box of ribbons and frowned at the contents. There was not enough of anything that could be used to re-hem one of Jane's dresses, but she could perhaps put together a new hair piece, or make some ribbon roses for the bodice or sleeves of one of her own dresses.

Jane pulled out a pale blue dress and held it up to her shoulders. "What do you think of this one?" she asked.

Elizabeth wrinkled her nose, but considered it carefully. "With a darker edging, perhaps purple, and a change to the length of the sleeves… Yes, I think it could be manageable," she replied.

"So plain," Jane lamented quietly, "but it will have to do. Darker ribbons it shall be."

Elizabeth nodded and pulled a few scraps of white ribbon from the box and laid them upon the coverlet. She had decided to make something for Jane's hair, instead.

"And what will you wear?" Jane asked suddenly.

"What shall *I* wear?" Elizabeth repeated. "Whyever would I need to—"

"You are coming with me to Netherfield Park," Jane said firmly.

"I— If you insist," she said upon seeing her sister's serious expression. "But I do not see why my presence would be necessary. If you are to go and make a good impression upon Mr. Bingley's sisters, you hardly need my assistance to do so!"

"But what of *your* impression upon Mr. Darcy?" Jane asked with a sly smile.

"Mr. Darcy?"

Elizabeth's cheeks warmed immediately at the mention of the gentleman's name. She had nearly forgotten that he was in residence at Netherfield Park… A visit to that house would mean the possibility of seeing him as well, and she did not deny that she would welcome such an opportunity.

Jane reached into the wardrobe and withdrew another dress, one that Elizabeth reserved for more elegant occasions. It was made of ivory muslin, with long sleeves, a high waistline, and a lower neckline than she would usually favor. "This one suits you very well, indeed," Jane said with some determination.

Elizabeth sighed dramatically but did not argue. She took the dress and laid it upon the bed.

"A violet ribbon would bring out the green in your eyes," Jane said wisely.

"Will you not use the violet for your own dress?" Elizabeth asked.

Jane nodded and smiled. "I shall use something else. But it is settled," she replied. "Come, we shall walk into Meryton together and set to our hemming as soon as possible."

Elizabeth could not hide her smile as she watched her sister move with singular purpose around the room as she prepared to leave the house. It did her heart good to see Jane happy, and if this was how she could participate in such happiness, she had no complaint to offer.

* * *

*M*eryton was crowded, but pleasantly so, and as Elizabeth and Jane moved through the cobbled streets, Elizabeth found herself in a remarkably jovial mood. Perhaps it was the prospect of seeing Mr. Darcy again. He had been a most agreeable dancing partner, and she had enjoyed her conversation with him... Indeed, how could she not be looking forward to continuing such an acquaintance?

Jane was radiant in her happiness, and Elizabeth did what she could to encourage it. They considered various topics of conversation which might be brought up at tea, and decided upon what questions to ask of Mr. Bingley's sisters—chiefly, how they were enjoying Hertfordshire as it compared to London.

It would certainly be different, but they had no other opinions to consider aside from that of their aunt, Mrs.

Gardiner, who often said that she preferred to come to the country to clear her head after so long in the city.

Elizabeth chose her purchases quickly, and while Jane lingered over the ribbons and lace, Elizabeth looked out the window of Mrs. Addison's shop at the people walking by. There were several familiar faces, but also new officers, and others she did not recognize. Meryton was growing by the year, and it would not be long before their quiet town would begin to feel crowded.

Such a change would suit Elizabeth very well, indeed, but she was not certain that her father would take kindly to having closer neighbors and navigate through larger crowds at market time, or on the rare occasions he came into town to see his solicitor.

As Jane selected her ribbons and signed her name into Mrs. Addison's credit book, Elizabeth spied another familiar face. "Jane," she said quickly. "Jane come and see, this is Mr. Wickham—the officer who came to Longbourn only the other day while you were out with Lydia and Kitty."

"I would have thought that they would return to speak to the girls," Jane said quietly as she came to the window to stand beside her sister. "We did not see them in town that day."

The officers were leaned against the wall of the Meryton Inn, engaged in casual conversation. Mr. Wickham's smile was broad as he laughed at something one of the officers had said.

"Should we speak to them?" Jane asked, but Elizabeth shook her head.

"I think not. They will come to see Lydia and Kitty if they are wont to do so, I shall not push on their behalf."

"Lydia would say that you are *very* unkind." Jane's tone was softly teasing and Elizabeth smiled.

"Perhaps I am," she said. "But Lydia is *very* silly to be entertaining the affections of *so* many officers at once."

"However will she choose? And what if they all propose marriage at once?" Jane's eyes sparkled with mirth and Elizabeth smothered her laughter with her hand as they exited the shop and stepped into the street.

"I refuse to believe that such a thing is possible. If Lydia receives a proposal of marriage before Mr. Bingley is down on one knee begging for your agreement to his own suit, I shall have to renounce all of my trust in divine justice, and love in general," Elizabeth declared.

"Oh, Lizzy, you are far too dramatic for such things," Jane said. She seemed about to say something more, but her words were cut off by the clatter of horseshoes upon the cobbles and she clutched Elizabeth's arm tightly as two gentlemen on horseback approached.

"Lizzy, it is Mr. Bingley," she hissed.

"And Mr. Darcy, too," Elizabeth observed. She also noted how fine he looked upon the back of the horse, and how comfortable in the saddle he seemed. The black gelding was responsive to every pressure of his legs and the movement of his hands upon the reins, making Mr. Bingley appear very stiff and ungainly in his own saddle by comparison.

"Miss Bennet," Mr. Bingley called out. "What a delight it is to see you in town!"

Jane greeted the gentlemen warmly and Elizabeth could see the happiness in her sister's eyes as she spoke to Mr. Bingley. But her own gaze was drawn to the dark haired gentlemen at his side.

Fitzwilliam Darcy smiled down at her and touched his fingers to the brim of his hat. He said nothing, but Elizabeth could feel her cheeks warm as she struggled to maintain her composure. She wanted to speak to him, but did not want to distract from Jane's conversation with Mr. Bingley.

"I am told that you have been invited to Netherfield Park for tea," Mr. Bingley said. "I do hope that it will not be an imposition upon your time, Caroline was *most* insistent upon the date."

"Oh, not at all," Jane said hastily. "I am thrilled, indeed, to have been invited. A reply was sent to Miss Bingley just before we departed for Meryton. You may assure her that we will be very pleased to attend."

"Delightful," Mr. Bingley said with a smile. Elizabeth could only confirm in her own mind that the gentleman's reaction was very much dependent upon his own chances of seeing Jane at Netherfield Park which had now increased.

"Lizzy will also be attending, of course," Jane said pointedly. Elizabeth glanced up at Mr. Darcy in surprise as Jane announced it. His eyebrows rose slightly, but he recovered himself and smiled, his expression mirroring that of his friend so quickly that Elizabeth barely noticed his hesitation.

"You will both be very welcome, indeed," Mr. Bingley said. "I am certain that Louisa and Caroline will be very glad of your company."

"No doubt," Mr. Darcy agreed, but his attention had been pulled away to the small group of officers who stood near the edge of the Meryton Inn. A few were holding flagons of ale, and their laughter was louder than it should have been for an early afternoon in late September.

"What is it?" Mr. Bingley asked. Elizabeth could sense his nervousness, as though his friend was not usually given to such distraction.

"Nothing," Mr. Darcy replied stiffly, but Elizabeth could see that was not the case. He was upset, but she could not determine why that might be. He recovered himself quickly and tightened his grip upon the reins. "Come, we must not keep these young ladies from their day. They will be at Netherfield Park soon enough and you may continue your conversations."

"Indeed," Mr. Bingley said as though he had finally understood his friend's reason for wanting to leave the streets. "I shall relay your message to my sisters, Miss Bennet, and shall await your arrival at Netherfield Park."

The gentlemen bid them goodbye and set their spurs into the flanks of their horses. As the horses' hooves clattered over the cobblestone street, Elizabeth finally realized what, or *whom*, Mr. Darcy had been staring at.

Mr. Wickham smiled at her from the corner of the White Horse Inn and raised his cup of ale in her direction. Elizabeth inclined her head slightly and then turned her attention to Jane.

"Did he not look handsome upon that horse, Lizzy?" Jane said breathlessly. "And to know that we are expected at Netherfield Park with all eagerness—"

"I am sorry, Jane," Elizabeth interrupted her sister's exuberance and laid a hand upon her arm. "Did you not notice how Mr. Darcy wanted to leave our company very suddenly?"

"I— He did," Jane said thoughtfully. "I wonder what it was that caused him to want to do so..."

Elizabeth's eyes caught Mr. George Wickham's again, and she straightened as she realized that he was moving through the crowd toward them.

"Jane," Elizabeth hissed.

"Oh," was the whispered reply as Jane recognized the officer from Elizabeth's words in Mrs. Addison's shop. There was no time to say anything further as the officer stopped before them and bowed.

"Miss Elizabeth Bennet," he said with a smile and then his eyes slid to Jane. "I do apologize, I do not know your companion."

"Mr. Wickham, this is my sister, Jane," Elizabeth said hastily. Jane nodded graciously, but just as she was about to say something, a friend of their mother's interrupted the conversation and pulled Jane away, leaving Elizabeth unexpectedly alone with the gentleman.

Mr. Wickham, however, seemed pleased by Jane's departure.

"Miss Bennet," he said, "might I ask you a question?"

Elizabeth smiled briefly and tucked her packet of ribbons under her arm. "Of course, Mr. Wickham. I trust that you are settling into your life here with the garrison?"

"I am, I thank you," he replied. But then he moved closer and lowered his voice. "I must ask... How well acquainted are you with Mr. Darcy?"

Elizabeth looked at him in surprise. "Mr. Darcy? Why, I do not know him well at all. He has only just arrived in Meryton with Mr. Bingley. We danced together at the assembly—"

"Did you? And did Mr. Bingley dance with your sister?"

Elizabeth raised a suspicious eyebrow. "He did, indeed," she replied.

"And what was your impression of the gentleman?"

"You are asking a great many questions, Mr. Wickham—" Elizabeth said briskly. She did not like his questions, though she could not say why that might have been. "What is it that you are trying to say?"

Mr. Wickham shook his head and smiled apologetically. "Please, you must forgive me, I am only enquiring with the very best of intentions. You see, I am somewhat acquainted with Mr. Darcy, and his... methods."

Elizabeth felt a small sting of suspicion in the back of her mind. "Methods?"

"Indeed. Mr. Darcy is well known for accommodating the requests of his friend, Mr. Bingley when wooing young ladies."

"Wooing?" Elizabeth blurted out.

"Perhaps I am being too blunt," Mr. Wickham said. "Mr. Bingley, when he finds a young lady that catches his interest, depends upon his friend Mr. Darcy to entertain the young lady closest to his intended..."

"What are you trying to say, Mr. Wickham? Speak plainly, or I shall have to take my leave of your company," she snapped. Elizabeth was becoming angry now. She did not like what Mr. Wickham was implying, but she needed to hear his accusation spoken in the most direct manner or not at all.

"You must forgive me," he said. "I am not certain of how best to explain this..."

"Explain it as plainly as you can," Elizabeth repeated. "I shall have to join my sister."

He smiled quickly. "Of course. It is only, I do not wish for you to feel slighted—"

"Slighted?" Elizabeth said. "And how would I feel anything such as that?"

Mr. Wickham looked uncomfortable, but only for a moment. "Mr. Darcy does not dance with young ladies to whom he feels any kind of affinity," he said. "He chooses his partners in accordance with what Mr. Bingley asks of him. He took a liking to your sister, and so, Mr. Darcy danced with you."

Elizabeth shook her head in confusion. "But... why?"

"What is your feeling toward Mr. Bingley?" he asked. "Favorable?"

"Yes... of course," Elizabeth answered carefully.

"And Mr. Darcy was charming, and an amiable partner on the dance floor?"

Mr. Wickham spoke as though he knew the gentleman and his 'methods,' as he called them, quite well.

"How do you know such things?" Elizabeth asked.

He shook his head ruefully. "I am truly sorry, Miss Bennet, but I am afraid that I have seen Mr. Darcy at work far too often. My own dear sister was once a victim of his wiles... He broke her heart most cruelly, and I would not see such a thing happen to the like of you."

"But, how—"

"Fitzwilliam Darcy *cannot* be considered a truthful man," Mr. Wickham said. His voice was hard and bitter as he spoke, and a shiver ran up Elizabeth's spine. "He pretends his affections, and then, when the young lady has truly lost her heart to him, he turns cold. He is the most cruel and unfeeling gentleman I have had the misfortune to meet."

Elizabeth's chest felt tight, and she shook her head, unwilling to believe that Mr. Darcy could have been false in his attentions toward her. But her immediate worry was for Jane.

"And Mr. Bingley?" she asked. "Is he not to be believed, either?"

Mr. Wickham shook his head. "No, I believe Mr. Bingley's intentions are sincere. Mr. Bingley is a good man, but I honestly cannot think of any reason why he should be such a good friend to Mr. Darcy—he certainly does not deserve such kindness."

Elizabeth felt a small moment of relief, but her anger surged once more against Mr. Darcy. *How dare he presume that he could deceive her in such a way—she would have discovered it before too long. Surely...*

"Lizzy," Jane called out. "Do come here—"

"I thank you for your warning, Mr. Wickham," she said.

"Miss Bennet—if you should see Mr. Darcy, do not tell him that it was I who alerted you to his treachery. He will suspect the worst, I am afraid, and I should not like to have him come looking for me..."

"I shall not betray your trust," Elizabeth said. "Thank you. Truly."

Mr. Wickham nodded and turned away to join the other officers once more and Elizabeth went to Jane's side and joined the conversation she was having with Mrs. Browning. She did her best to contribute to the discussion, but found that her mind wandered far too often to Mr. Darcy and what Mr. Wickham had said about him. *Could he really be false in his attentions to her?*

He had seemed sincere, and Elizabeth had thought—

No. She could not think of such things. She should not have hoped for such an impossibility.

Whatever Mr. Darcy had intended to accomplish, he had been successful. Jane was well and truly on her way to being in love with Mr. Bingley, and Elizabeth did not want to put her sister's happiness in any danger.

If she confronted Mr. Darcy, and he admitted the truth— would Jane lose Mr. Bingley's affections forever? Or if she told Jane of what Mr. Wickham had said, would she even believe it? Elizabeth, herself, was struggling to make sense of what the officer had said... It did not make any sense for him to lie, but Elizabeth did not know what to believe.

4

"*L*izzy, you are so distracted this morning," Jane said with a sigh as she tied the ribbon of her bonnet under her chin.

"You must forgive me," Elizabeth said. "I have no excuse. I am certain I shall be myself again once we begin our walk. I did not sleep well."

She hoped that her words would reassure her sister, but it was true that she was struggling to summon any enthusiasm for their walk to Netherfield Park.

The day was fine, and though Mrs. Bennet would not cease vocalizing her hopes for a rain storm that would keep them at Netherfield Park at least until supper time, it did not seem as though the weather would cooperate with her plans.

"What do you think Miss Bingley and Mrs. Hurst will be like?" Jane asked.

"I cannot say. But I do hope that there are raspberry tarts at tea," Elizabeth murmured. She wanted to do her best to distract her sister from any nervousness she might have, but masking her own discomfort with the situation would be difficult.

"You will promise to ask about Mr. Bingley," Mrs. Bennet

said as she walked with them through the courtyard. "There is no inopportune time to present yourself as the very best option for his future happiness!"

"Yes, Mama," Jane replied dutifully.

Elizabeth merely shook her head and took Jane's arm to lead her away from the house while their mother waved her handkerchief and called out admonishments and reminders.

"She will not be happy until all of us are properly married," Jane said with a sigh.

"Properly?" Elizabeth laughed. "She would be happy for us to be married to whomever would take us, so long as we were out of the house as quickly as possible."

"Lizzy," Jane gasped. "You do not believe that to be true. Surely!"

Elizabeth shook her head, suddenly tired of mirth. "No, indeed. I know she has the best of intentions... It just seems as though her obsession with our marital status has become an all-consuming search for any gentleman who might be even slightly suitable. I daresay she would even allow Mary to run away with any young man who comes to call."

"Mary?" Jane laughed. "If any gentleman comes calling for Mary, I do believe Mama would die of shock before she could make any measurements for her wedding gown."

It seemed a sad thing to laugh about, but Mary did not seem to have the slightest interest in seeking out any such gentleman. For his part, Mr. Bennet seemed content with such things, but their mother would not be deterred. But however much Mrs. Bennet wished for all of her daughters to be married and secure, Elizabeth suspected that it would be a long time before Mary showed any enthusiasm for their mother's schemes.

· · ·

The walk to Netherfield Park was a pleasant one, and Elizabeth was almost reluctant to take the turn that would lead them toward Netherfield Park. She did not want to run the risk of seeing Mr. Darcy—if she had worried about what she would say to him before Mr. Wickham's revelation, she had even more cause to worry now. There was no way to know what might happen, and the chance that her anger and frustration might overtake her manners was very likely. If she could not control her emotions, she would, no doubt, say something she would regret.

"I daresay I do not ever think I shall be able to see myself living in such a grand house," Jane said as they approached Netherfield Park.

The wide road was lined with slender birch trees, and the sweet sound of birdsong accompanied their steps.

"Perhaps you should begin to imagine yourself here," Elizabeth said warmly. "It will make the reality of it far easier to bear."

"You sound almost as certain as our dear Mama," Jane laughed.

Elizabeth did not reply, but reached out to squeeze her sister's hand briefly. She had no choice but to believe that Mr. Bingley was sincere in his affections toward her sister.

Her complaint was not with him.

It was with Mr. Darcy.

Jane seemed to be in a great hurry, and Elizabeth encouraged her to go ahead. "My boot has come loose," Elizabeth said. "Go on, I shall join you presently."

Jane did not hesitate long before turning back toward Netherfield's front doors as Elizabeth bent to refasten the buckle on her boot.

"Miss Elizabeth Bennet… I did not expect to see you in the grass."

Elizabeth straightened quickly and tried to ignore the headache that sprang up behind her eyes as she did so.

Her cheeks warmed immediately as Mr. Fitzwilliam Darcy, dressed in a fine dark coat and a well-tailored waistcoat that fit snugly around his torso, strode through the garden toward her.

She fought the urge to frown, and then tried to smooth her features so as not to betray her true feelings—Jane often chided her for wearing her emotions so plainly, but such a thing could not be helped in every instance.

"Mr. Darcy," she said in as neutral a tone she could manage. "A surprise, to be sure. I shall not keep you… my sister will be waiting for me to join her. We are here to see Miss Bingley and Mrs. Hurst for tea."

The gentleman's eyebrow rose slightly. "Your sister seems to have abandoned you," he observed.

He looked past her toward the front doors, and Elizabeth looked over her shoulder to do the same—she had expected to see Jane waiting for her upon the stairs, but the door was closed and Jane was nowhere to be seen.

She had not waited—not even for a moment.

Elizabeth pressed her lips together and looked back at Mr. Darcy. His dark eyes held hers for a moment before looking away and Elizabeth felt a familiar anger flare briefly in her chest.

"Indeed," she said. "As I said, I shall not keep you. I am certain that you have much more important matters to attend to," she said stiffly.

Mr. Darcy inclined his head, and Elizabeth was almost disappointed that he did not argue with her. In her mind, his reaction only solidified what Mr. Wickham had said. She was about to take her leave of him, but then her desire to know the truth fought its way through her better judgement.

"Mr. Darcy," she said. "Might I ask how it is that you are acquainted with Mr. Wickham?"

The gentleman paused, and Elizabeth thought she saw anger in his eyes before his expression became one of disinterest. "I had some acquaintance with the man in my younger days," he said. "He is not a man to be trusted, and I do hope that you have not—"

"Have not given him more trust than I should have?" Elizabeth interrupted him. "I have spoken with him… And he told me some very troubling news."

"And what was that?"

"That *I* should not trust *you*," Elizabeth retorted.

"Indeed."

Elizabeth fumed for a moment as she waited for him to ask what she meant by such a bold statement, but he said nothing.

Finally, Elizabeth could take the silence no longer.

"I must know the truth," she blurted out. "At the assembly. Did you ask me to dance because you *wanted* to dance with me, or because you wanted me to speak kindly of Mr. Bingley to my sister?"

Mr. Darcy blinked at her for a moment, then he shook his head and chuckled softly. "Why, Miss Elizabeth Bennet. Have I offended your pride?"

Elizabeth's mouth fell open in surprise. "I beg your pardon?"

"Mr. Bingley admired your sister greatly, and wished to dance with her. I helped him by distracting you… and if that had caused you, in turn, to speak kindly of him in private, then there is no harm in it. In the end, your sister is the one who benefits from your wounded pride."

"Benefits?" Elizabeth spluttered.

"Indeed," Mr. Darcy replied in a casual tone. "Mr. Bingley

seems to have developed some genuine affection for her. So, I thank you for whatever you have said to encourage your sister's affections. Or, perhaps Charles should thank you."

"You... You are a charlatan!" Elizabeth said hotly.

Mr. Darcy's smile was wry as he crossed his arms over his chest. "I am nothing if not an honest man, Miss Bennet," he said. "I have only done what I have been asked. No more, no less."

"I— I..."

But Elizabeth did not know what to say. In fact, she could not decide if she was furious, upset, hurt, or a mixture of all three. She hated him. She wanted to strike him. She wanted to run away...

But she was frozen in place and he would not take that infuriating smile off his face.

In fact, her discomfort seemed to amuse him even more.

"You must promise me something, Miss Bennet," he said suddenly.

"How dare—"

"You must promise me that you will say nothing to your sister of your hurt feelings—I have no doubt she would feel obligated to support you in your anger—"

"As any good sister should," Elizabeth snapped.

"Indeed, but in so doing you would, no doubt, ruin your sister's chances at a happy, and profitable, marriage. Surely, you are aware of Mr. Bingley's income."

"Of course I am," Elizabeth replied. "And yours."

"Gossip is reliable in that respect," he said with a rueful chuckle. "I hardly think that in a place such as Hertfordshire that such a good match would present itself again. Could you forgive yourself if your sister were unable to find such happiness again? Considering the quality of officer that seems to populate the militia garrison, I suspect not."

Elizabeth's cheeks burned with embarrassment and anger.

"Mr. Darcy," she said stiffly. "If you are quite finished? You have managed to insult me in so many areas that I know not which to be angriest about."

He stepped closer, and Elizabeth flinched as he took hold of her wrist and held it gently. "Do I have your promise, then?"

Elizabeth fumed for a moment, but then nodded. "You do," she said. "But do not think to speak to me about *anything*. Not even the weather, or the quality of the music, nor any other innocuous topic that should spring to mind..."

She pulled her wrist out of his grasp easily and clenched her hand into a fist at her side.

Mr. Darcy nodded his agreement. "As you wish," he said.

"I do," she replied hotly.

Without another word, Elizabeth turned and strode toward the house. Her cheeks burned and she knew that she would have to work diligently to compose herself before she was presented to Miss Bingley and Mrs. Hurst, but this information would be a burden she would have to bear alone. Jane could never know what had happened. It did not affect her in the slightest. If Mr. Darcy was correct in his assumption, then Mr. Bingley *did* have true affection for her sister. She could not stand in the way of that.

As she walked up the front steps of Netherfield Park, Elizabeth looked over her shoulder, back toward the gardens, but Mr. Darcy had disappeared around the corner of the house. The door opened before she could lift the knocker and Elizabeth smiled as the face of an older man appeared in the doorway.

"I do apologize, I believe I am late for tea," she said.

"Miss Bennet," the man said warmly. "You are expected. Come this way."

Elizabeth stepped through the door and took a deep breath

to calm herself as she tried to think of a reason for her tardiness that she could offer to her hostesses.

The butler led her down a long corridor and gestured toward an open door. She could hear feminine laughter inside the room and she took another breath before she smoothed down her skirts, thanked the man, and stepped through the door.

5

Nothing could have prepared Elizabeth for taking tea with Miss Caroline Bingley and Mrs. Louisa Hurst. Where Mr. Bingley seemed to be an amiable man in possession of a good temperament and a fine senseability about him, his sisters were *quite* the opposite.

Mrs. Hurst had married for money, and it was clear in how she spoke of her husband that she loathed the sight of him. This came as no surprise; Elizabeth, and every other person with eyes who had attended the Meryton assembly, had observed how Mr. Bingley's sisters had barely tolerated Mr. Hurst's company. Elizabeth could only wonder at how such a marriage might be borne by either party, but she did not dare ask such a thing.

While Louisa Hurst was filled with bitterness and unhappy discord, Miss Caroline Bingley was a viper in a silk dress. She fawned over Jane and laid many compliments in her lap, but Elizabeth could not shake her suspicion that such honeyed words were only a thin veneer to cover the other woman's shrewd judgements. She could sense a sort of cruelty behind Caroline's questions about their family and their life in

Hertfordshire, and Elizabeth could only hope that her sister was wise enough to see through such a false pageantry of friendship.

For a woman of considerable accomplishment, Caroline Bingley's questions and replies to Jane's conversation were vapid and careless, and Elizabeth began to feel insulted by the barely concealed condescension in Caroline's tone.

Thankfully, Jane seemed unaffected by all of it, and Elizabeth was grateful that her sister was in possession of such a sweet soul and seemed happy to answer all of Miss Bingley's questions, no matter how strange they might have been.

Elizabeth could only hope that suffering through this tea would mean that Jane would have a greater chance of securing some support for the affection she had for Mr. Bingley. Sisters could be great allies, but they could also be the deadliest of foes. She knew that there was nothing she could say to the contrary. Her pride had been hurt, to be sure, but that should not affect Jane.

*E*lizabeth battled with her guilt and anger for weeks while Jane continued to receive invitations to Netherfield Park for tea with Mr. Bingley's sisters.

Miss Bingley and Mrs. Hurst did not come to Longbourn, though not for lack of invitation. There was always some excuse or other as to why they could not leave Netherfield Park, and soon enough, Jane stopped asking.

However much his sisters avoided Longbourn, Mr. Bingley did come for supper on more than one occasion. Each subsequent visit sent Mrs. Bennet into fits of hopeful joy that a proposal would be coming sooner rather than later.

But Elizabeth could not trust such a thing. She only hoped that Mr. Darcy had kept his own counsel and had not convinced his friend to abandon his interest in her sister as punishment for Elizabeth's anger during their confrontation in the garden.

She had been on the edge of a knife for weeks, unable to enjoy any activities or suppers for fear that Jane would receive word that an invitation to tea had been cancelled, or that Mr. Bingley would *not* be joining them for supper. But no such letter ever arrived and Elizabeth began to relax.

The weather turned quickly, and the crisp mornings of late autumn became cold and damp, and the almanac's threats of snow began to seem more and more likely with each passing day.

On the first day of December, an unexpected letter arrived, addressed to all of the Bennet family.

Lydia, of course, opened it and Elizabeth watched with half-distracted interest as her youngest sister had ripped open the seal and unfolded the thick paper. Lydia's eyes widened as she read the words upon the page, but it had not taken long for Mrs. Bennet to grow tired of her daughter's shocked gasps and desperate noises.

"Oh, Lydia, do cease your moaning," Mrs. Bennet said. She snatched the letter from Lydia's hands, snapped the paper free of its creases, and cleared her throat before reading aloud:

> *To the Bennet Family,*
>
> *Greetings from Netherfield Park,*
>
> *You are, one and all, cordially invited to attend a Christmas ball.*
>
> *To be held upon the second Thursday of December.*

"And it is signed with Mr. Bingley's own hand!" Lydia cried. "A Christmas ball! Did I not say, Kitty! Did I not *say* that Mr. Bingley would be *sure* to host a ball of his own?"

"Yes, Lydia," Kitty admitted in a somewhat dejected tone.

"The second Thursday of December," Mrs. Bennet mused. Elizabeth wondered if her mother might try to find some reason to reply to the invitation with notice that they would be giving up some other 'important event' to be there. Mrs. Bennet lived for drama, and she did not seem to shy away from creating some where it did not exist just to entertain herself.

"I seem to recall that your aunt—"

"Mama, there is no other invitation," Elizabeth said sharply. Jane's glance was filled with caution and Elizabeth bit her lip. She had not meant to sound so forceful, but they all knew that there was no other engagement on that day. No doubt, Miss Bingley had chosen it specifically for that reason. It was early enough in the month that there should be no other Christmastide obligations, for the majority of the families in Hertfordshire made all of their plans for Christmas Day and the week following. There would be a regimental ball hosted by Colonel Forster before the new year arrived, but nothing that would compete with a ball at Netherfield Park.

"Quite right, Lizzy," Mrs. Bennet replied with a sigh. "I shall send our reply at once."

Kitty and Lydia's happy cries echoed through the house as Mrs. Bennet sent them to fetch her writing box, and Jane could not stop smiling.

"A Christmas ball, how wonderful. And I am almost certain that Mr. Bingley will offer a proposal to Jane—what better time to do so?" Mrs. Bennet beamed at her eldest daughter, who blushed prettily at the suggestion. Elizabeth knew that Jane had been hoping for that very event to occur, but she would never expect it... that was their mother's current obsession. "All of my friends say that it will come sooner than later. It is inevitable." She sounded so very certain, but Elizabeth could not allow herself to hope. Only when the words had been spoken by the gentleman himself would she believe that it was true.

"Mama," Elizabeth said quietly. She could only make an attempt to quiet her mother's one-sided conversation, but also knew that it was almost impossible to do.

"The gentleman is by now most certainly in love with her," Mrs. Bennet continued. "It seems only *natural* that such a thing should happen. Besides, he will not find a young woman as accomplished or as beautiful as our Jane!"

"Mama," Elizabeth said again through gritted teeth. Mrs. Bennet waved her away and held the letter aloft as she flounced over to her writing desk. Kitty and Lydia's argument over who would carry their mother's writing box echoed down the corridor and Elizabeth gritted her teeth in frustration.

Everything was an argument with those girls.

Jane squeezed Elizabeth's arm gently and leaned closer. "What a wonderful surprise," she said.

"It is, indeed," Elizabeth agreed. "But I do hope that you will not feel disappointed if—"

"If a proposal does not come?" Jane finished her sentence and nodded briefly. "Of course, I have considered it. But I have reason to hope that I can find my happiness. Miss Bingley and Mrs. Hurst have assured me that they would be very glad to call me sister."

Elizabeth did not trust such talk, but she could only smile at her sister's genuine belief that Mr. Bingley's sisters wished her well.

But none of that mattered. The house was filled with excitement over the invitation, and Elizabeth could not help but be swept up in it all. Kitty and Lydia laughed and talked of what they would wear to the ball while Mrs. Bennet wrote out their reply. Elizabeth folded her hands in her lap as Jane smiled and joined in the lively conversation. Jane had no worries about the ball, it was only she who would have to hope that fortune would be on her side. When the evening of the ball arrived, she could only hope that she would be able to keep her promise and avoid Mr. Fitzwilliam Darcy entirely.

*T*he days passed quickly, and with each one the shadow of Elizabeth's dread lengthened just a little more. Jane's invitations to take tea at Netherfield continued to arrive, but Elizabeth would only attend if Jane requested her presence.

On one such day, a mere three days before the ball was to be held, a light snow had begun to fall, and Miss Bingley had been kind enough to send a carriage to collect them.

"See that you ask Miss Bingley if she requires any assistance with the decorations for the ball," Mrs. Bennet cried from the doorway as they stepped up into the carriage.

"Of course, Mama," Jane replied.

"Do you really believe that Miss Bingley would ask for any assistance with her decor?" Elizabeth asked as they brushed the snow from their shawls and pulled a fur rug over their knees.

Jane settled back against the seat and sighed. "Indeed, I do not. But we must tell Mama that Miss Bingley will consider it."

"We will certainly not be asking her such a thing."

Jane grimaced but did not argue. There was no sense in putting their reputation in any danger by pushing their mother's assumptions and agenda upon the situation.

Elizabeth steeled herself for another interaction with Mr. Bingley's sisters. It was obvious to her that the other women merely tolerated her presence at Netherfield Park, but she could not say anything to Jane as her sister seemed to genuinely enjoy her time with Caroline and Louisa. Or, at the very least, she had said nothing against them.

Elizabeth was fully prepared to defend her sister should the need arise, but she hoped that she would not have to.

"Has Miss Bingley said anything to you about her brother's intentions?" Elizabeth asked as the carriage rolled away from Longbourn. She had asked this of her sister before, but Jane had never had an answer.

Her sister sighed heavily, but then smiled. "Not in so many words, but Miss Bingley has been very kind to me, and I have no reason to believe that she would do so if her brother were not interested in pursuing such a—"

Jane paused and looked down at her hands.

"Such a course of action?" Elizabeth guessed.

"Yes. Precisely that," Jane said with a small smile.

"I envy you, Jane," Elizabeth said. "You seem so very happy, and I hope that I might be able to find the same sort of happiness for myself."

"Oh, Lizzy, I am certain that you will!"

Elizabeth shook her head as an image of Mr. Darcy's face flashed before her eyes. Anger swelled in her chest and she could not find the positivity that she normally would have been able to summon in such a situation. The revelation of Mr. Darcy's deception was still raw, and though she had hoped her anger would have faded over time, it had not.

"I believe I have asked too much," Elizabeth said with some bitterness. "You have heard me say on far too many occasions that only the very deepest love could have tempted *me* into an agreement of marriage... But I have been foolish in my assertions. I am not so certain that such a thing exists for me."

"It is not like you to be so defeated," Jane murmured.

"Perhaps it is the weather," Elizabeth said but her smile felt tight instead of reassuring. "Do not worry for me, Jane, you have more important things to think about than the state of my heart."

Jane laid a hand upon her sister's and squeezed it gently. "I shall always worry for you, Lizzy," she said.

The carriage turned up the wide dirt road that led toward Netherfield Park, and Elizabeth did not reply. There would be enough to distract her from her own thoughts at Netherfield Park, of that she was certain.

***

"Now, Miss Eliza," Caroline Bingley said, airily, "you really *must* tell me how the young ladies of Hertfordshire hope to find good husbands—it does seem a terrible waste of accomplishment for all of these young women to marry officers of the militia."

It was clear from Mrs. Hurst's laughter that Caroline Bingley's words were meant to be humorous, but Elizabeth failed to see how such a thing could be possible. Her aim was to insult not just Elizabeth and her sisters, but the whole of Meryton and Hertfordshire in one simple turn of phrase.

"And how would such a thing be a waste?" Elizabeth asked. "I should prefer such a match over a gentleman who would expect his wife to perform like a caged bird at every opportunity."

Jane coughed lightly and sipped at her tea.

"Sing, darling! Our guests are waiting!" Elizabeth exclaimed mockingly. Jane smiled—it was a joke they had often spoken of in private, but Elizabeth had never had the opportunity to make her opinion known in public before. She knew that she should not have said such a thing, but, as was often the case, her words had rushed out before she could stop herself.

Caroline Bingley smiled thinly and reached across the couch

to pat her sister's hand. "Do not despair, Louisa," she said. "Miss Eliza has every right to say such things. It is often the way of the unaccomplished to mock that which they do not possess in order to take focus away from their own shortcomings. I daresay that she would be delighted *not* to be asked to perform."

Elizabeth returned Miss Bingley's smile and tapped her spoon upon the edge of her teacup smartly. "Indeed not, I should not wish to bring any shame upon my husband with a poor performance. And I would never wish such a thing upon my guests—it would deprive them of the pleasure of my conversation, which is, most assuredly, more enjoyable than my pianoforte playing."

Elizabeth thought she heard a noise in the corridor, but when she turned to look, there was nothing to be seen.

"I shall be sure not to command you to perform for us," Mrs, Hurst said stiffly.

"I thank you," Elizabeth replied. "It would be more for your own benefit that I stay silent at such gatherings."

"Which seems a fantasy, indeed," Caroline sniped as she poured another cup of tea for herself.

"Have you engaged musicians for the ball?" Jane interrupted, changing the subject deftly so as to avoid any further disagreement or awkwardness.

Elizabeth had made her decision on her opinion of Miss Bingley many months ago, but with every interaction her impression of the other woman was solidified all the more. She did not know why Jane seemed intent on expressing her delight at the possibility of calling these two snakes 'sister,' but it seemed more and more likely that Jane was hoping for a cordial relationship with Mr. Bingley's sisters should she become mistress of Netherfield Park.

It seemed like a desperate wish. But Jane had always been impossibly optimistic.

"We have, indeed," Caroline replied confidently. "Our friends in London have been instrumental in assisting us with choosing musicians who will be able to perform all of the music that we require for the evening."

"Our brother has been kind enough to indulge all of our requests for entertainment and food," Mrs. Hurst said with what Elizabeth could only surmise was a smug expression upon her face.

"The food as well?" Elizabeth asked.

"Oh, yes," Louisa sniffed. "Ingredients and chefs from London will be brought in... I cannot abide this... country fare."

"Indeed," Elizabeth said softly.

"You may assure your younger sisters that we have invited Colonel Forster and instructed him to bring only the most *promising* of his young officers," Louisa continued. "There will be no shortage of dancing partners, and you can be certain that they will be of the highest quality."

"Very kind," Elizabeth said dryly.

There was another sound beyond the parlor door, and when Elizabeth turned her head to see what it was, she thought she saw a figure in the corridor. Listening at the door.

"Is Mr. Bingley in the house today," she asked suddenly. Mr. Bingley was rarely present when Jane came to Netherfield Park, and Elizabeth could only guess that his sisters had been working diligently to keep him and Jane apart—for what reason she could not guess, for Mr. Bingley's affection for Jane seemed not to have been dimmed by their absence from one another.

"He is not," Caroline replied briskly. "He has been called away to London."

"But he will return before the ball," Jane said. "Surely."

Caroline Bingley exchanged a look with her sister and Elizabeth narrowed her eyes briefly.

"It is difficult to say," Louisa said. "He did not tell us when he would be returning."

"I cannot imagine that he would not attend his own ball," Elizabeth said.

Caroline's smile did not reach all the way to her pale blue eyes and Elizabeth trusted her even less than she had before.

"Perhaps you are correct," Caroline said casually. "Charles can be quite punctual when he means to be."

Out of the corner of her eye, Elizabeth saw her sister relax just a little. She had to be content with their explanation, any argument or pressing for more details would only upset Jane, and that was the very last thing Elizabeth wanted.

Mr. Bingley's absence, if he was, indeed, absent, was worrisome enough for both of them—though for very different reasons.

"You must tell us about your plans for the decorations," Jane said after a moment. "Mama has been speculating for days. The ballroom is so large, however do you plan to do it?"

Elizabeth looked down at her tea while Caroline and Louisa gave vague answers to Jane's questions. She was not listening to their conversation, but was thinking about the noise she had heard in the corridor. Mr. Bingley might have been in London, but no one had mentioned where Mr. Darcy was. If he was in the house, could he have been listening to their conversation?

And if he had, would he have found her opinions on accomplishment humorous or insulting... *But why would she care what he thought?* If she did care, it would be with the hope that, if he *had* been listening, that he would be insulted by such talk. He seemed to her to be *precisely* the sort of gentleman who would demand that his wife perform for their guests, if only so that he would not have to speak overmuch.

"Miss Eliza," Caroline said, "do you find something amusing?"

Elizabeth looked up from her tea. "Oh, no. No, indeed," she replied. "Please, continue."

Caroline Bingley shook her head minutely and Louisa took a deep breath and continued to speak about the pine branches and winter flowers that would decorate Netherfield Park's ballroom and Elizabeth stopped listening once more.

She would endure many things to ensure Jane's happiness, but teatime with Mr. Bingley's sisters was quickly becoming her least favorite activity.

6

———

"*I* cannot help but feel somewhat strange," Jane said. Elizabeth slid a final pin into her sister's hair. "Strange?"

Jane sighed heavily, but then turned her head to smile at Elizabeth. "I have never been... So *unsettled* before a ball."

"Oh, Jane... It is only natural," Elizabeth said. "Mama has been relentless in her talk of engagements and weddings— But you must not think of that now."

"Then what must I think about instead?" Jane asked. Her voice was full of frustration, but Elizabeth did not know what counsel to offer. If she could have found a way to accomplish such a thing, she would have happily stayed home while the rest of the family went to Netherfield Park.

The knowledge that she might see Mr. Wickham in attendance was the only spark of interest that she could find in what would surely be an evening of stiff interactions and a steadfast avoidance of Mr. Fitzwilliam Darcy.

Elizabeth smiled and laid a reassuring hand upon her sister's shoulder. "I believe you should concentrate on nothing more than your steps, and ensure that you are available to dance with

Mr. Bingley whenever he asks. In fact, *I* believe you should dance with every gentleman or officer who comes within reach!"

"That sounds like advice *Lydia* would give," Jane laughed, "not you!"

"Perhaps it is," Elizabeth admitted. "But it shall surely keep you distracted from whatever strangeness you might be feeling... And will keep you as far away from Mama and her machinations as possible."

"A very difficult feat, indeed," Jane sighed.

"But an enjoyable avoidance, at least," Elizabeth said with a smile.

"At the very least."

The sisters laughed together briefly, but their mirth was cut short by their mother's shout from the foyer.

"Come now, Jane," Elizabeth said brightly. "We have been summoned."

Jane sighed and examined her hair in the vanity mirror before she rose from her chair. She took the gloves that Elizabeth held out for her and draped her shawl over her arm.

"We have, indeed," she replied.

Sir William had come to Longbourn earlier in the evening to collect Mr. Bennet, but the carriage carrying the female members of the Bennet household arrived not long after.

Even before the carriage drew to a halt in Netherfield Park's courtyard, Lydia and Kitty tumbled out with excited shouts upon their lips and ran through the light dusting of snow toward the open front doors. Mrs. Bennet, too, seemed in brighter spirits than she had been in many months, and Elizabeth could only hope that such a mood would continue after the revelries had faded.

Elizabeth and Jane took a more sedate pace, taking in as much of the sight of the house as they could. Every tall window of Netherfield Park's main floor blazed with candlelight and large lamps had been set upon the wide window ledges.

Elizabeth took a deep breath as they walked up the stone steps and entered Netherfield Park's large foyer.

The entryway had been swagged with fresh pine boughs, bright red berries, and long white ribbons, the sight of which gave Elizabeth cause for a genuine smile.

"How beautiful," Jane breathed.

"I have no doubt that every one of Lady Lucas' dinner parties will be decorated in a similar manner for the next year," Elizabeth said quietly.

Jane struggled not to laugh as they walked down the corridor behind their mother and sisters.

Elizabeth's resistance to coming to Netherfield Park reared up again as they stepped into the ballroom.

Caroline Bingley and Louisa Hurst's decorating far surpassed anything that had yet

been seen in Hertfordshire and Elizabeth felt very out of place in the opulent room. A feeling which she was certain had been purposefully orchestrated. She could see others in the room who looked equally uncomfortable, but they were hiding it well.

Musicians played with gusto, but the tune, and the dance, was unfamiliar, and Elizabeth could see confusion on the faces of her younger sisters as they struggled to keep up with the steps. The other couples on the dance floor were, very obviously, not from Hertfordshire. *London friends come to the country to gawk at the locals and sample a simpler fare, no doubt.*

Elizabeth's bitter thoughts were interrupted as Mr. Bingley appeared through the crowd and bowed gracefully to them.

"Miss Bennet," he greeted them warmly. "I do hope that you have not promised your dance card to anyone else?"

A blush painted Jane's cheeks almost immediately. "We have only just arrived," she said. "I have not yet had the opportunity to do so."

"I believe, sister, that you will have no need of a dance card this evening," Elizabeth murmured. Despite the pang she felt at willingly following Mr. Darcy's plan to be used as an encouragement to her sister's affection for Mr. Bingley, she pushed Jane gently toward the gentleman. She would do anything for Jane—even if it included the sacrifice of her own pride for her sister's sake. Jane could never know. All she needed to worry about was Mr. Bingley's affection, which, to Elizabeth, seemed unmarred by anything his sisters might have said about Jane behind closed doors.

Jane might have believed the best of Caroline and Louisa; but Elizabeth was not so trusting, and she was determined to keep a sharp eye on the gentleman's sisters for any sign of treachery. Especially now.

Jane smiled and laid her hand upon Mr. Bingley's proffered elbow. "Lizzy, will you be—"

Elizabeth pushed her sister gently toward the dance floor. "I shall be very well, indeed. Now, go and dance with this fine gentleman!"

Jane laughed and did as she was directed and Elizabeth caught a grateful nod from Mr. Bingley as they moved through the crowd toward the dance floor.

"Why, Miss Eliza Bennet."

Elizabeth recognized Caroline Bingley's smoothly condescending voice instantly and her fingers gripped the edge of her gown tightly as she struggled to find some politeness to offer the evening's hostess.

"Miss Bingley," Elizabeth said. "Thank you for your invitation to the ball. You have done a marvel with this room."

Caroline Bingley looked briefly at the decor and a small smile played upon her thin lips. "It is rather lovely, is it not? A pity that we were not able to locate the proper flowers, but we must make do here in the country. In London this would have been a very different affair. But one cannot have everything one desires."

"Indeed," Elizabeth said. She did not know how else to reply. It seemed that every word that came out of Caroline's mouth held an edge of judgement, or a challenge of some kind. Elizabeth supposed that would be a very difficult way to live one's life.

"You sisters have all taken to the dance floor," Caroline observed.

"Yes. Lydia and Kitty are drawn to dancing as ducks to water," Elizabeth said.

Caroline's smile was cold as her gaze roamed over the dancing couples. "Indeed. Let us hope that they grow into swans sooner than later."

Elizabeth could hear the condescension in Caroline's words, but decided against a sharp retort. "I see my friend Charlotte Lucas has arrived," Elizabeth said stiffly. "If you will excuse me."

"Of course. Do not tarry too long, Miss Eliza, you may find that all of the accomplished partners have already become engaged and will no longer have need of you."

Elizabeth turned away from Caroline Bingley's catlike smile and false manners and walked quickly through the crowd toward the banquet tables. She had, unfortunately, not seen Charlotte yet, but any excuse that would have served the purpose of escaping from Miss Bingley's company would have been ideal.

In Charlotte's absence, Elizabeth acquired a glass of punch and a sweet tart to help her forget her anger. She had not come to Netherfield Park with the intention of being angry, and she would not allow Caroline Bingley to ruin the evening so soon after it had begun.

She had enough to worry about as it was.

To calm herself further while she sipped her punch, Elizabeth tried to focus on the fashions that were on display and the society that was reflected in the guests who had been invited. It was obvious to any observer that many of the people in the ballroom were not from Hertfordshire. *A sampling of Caroline Bingley's London friends,* Elizabeth thought.

Fine dresses in a rainbow of colors and rich fabrics paired with elaborate hair ornaments for the women. Expensively tailored suits. embroidered waistcoats, and highly polished leather boots for the gentlemen. These people wore their wealth on the outside and had no qualms about it.

Even if she were to speak to any of them, what could she possibly have in common with these ladies? She could already hear their questions as to her accomplishments and why she was not married yet.

Elizabeth drank the last of the punch and set her glass down upon the table, she would have to be careful not to drink too much—she had heard too many stories about other young ladies who had become too drunk and acted inappropriately, and if there was one thing she had learned from her mother's penchant for gossip, it was that not having one's name mentioned after the evening had ended was a very good thing.

After only a moment of standing alone, Elizabeth was pleased to accept the request for a dance from a dashing officer whom she had not met before. His conversation was light and pleasant, but Elizabeth could not decide if he was interesting, or if her attraction to him was based solely upon the fact that he was taller than any other gentleman she had recently danced with.

As the dance ended, she turned away from her partner to look for Jane and Mr. Bingley, and smiled as she saw the gentleman steal a moment to kiss Jane's gloved hand briefly.

One day, I shall find a gentleman who causes me to smile as Jane is now, she thought.

The final bars of the song rang through the room and Elizabeth turned back to her partner, whose name she had all but forgotten, and froze in place. Standing in place of the tall officer was the very gentleman she had wanted to avoid.

"Mr. Darcy," she choked out.

"Miss Elizabeth Bennet."

The first notes of another dance began and Elizabeth looked around desperately for the officer, but he seemed to have disappeared into the crowd.

Mr. Darcy bowed and Elizabeth had no choice but to curtsey as the other couples began to move around them.

"Your hand, Miss Bennet," he said.

Elizabeth's cheeks burned as she placed her hand in his and tried desperately to focus on her steps.

"I expect you are surprised to see me here," he said as they came together.

"No," Elizabeth replied swiftly. "I would not expect you to be absent from such an event. Surely there would be more opportunity to dance with a young lady who could further your ambitions. There are several here that I do not recognize. Perhaps one of them would be more to your preference?"

"My preference," he said with some measure of surprise. "And what would you know of such a thing?"

Elizabeth was flustered, she had not meant— *What a horrid man to twist her words.*

"I—"

Mr. Darcy smiled as they parted to allow another couple to pass by, and when he took her hand again he stared into her eyes with such an intensity that Elizabeth could not help but look away.

"I must confess something to you, Miss Bennet," he said.

Elizabeth looked at him suspiciously. She was not prepared to trust much of what he might say to her. Especially after what she had learned from Mr. Wickham, and what Mr. Darcy had already confessed to her in the gardens beside Netherfield Park.

"You have already confessed too much," Elizabeth said tartly.

"I suppose I have earned your ire," he said simply, "and I am certain that there are many more things that I will do that will be deserving of chastisement before my life is over... However, I must tell you this one thing."

"And what might that be?" Elizabeth did not know if she wanted to hear what he had to say, but she was trapped upon the dance floor with him, and there would be no escape until the dance was over—if she left his side now, there would be gossip, and questions that she did not relish answering.

"Do you often receive compliments on your opinions, Miss Bennet?" he asked.

"Compliments?" Elizabeth asked in surprise. "I am sure I do not know what you mean."

"Your ideas... I particularly enjoyed your opinion on female accomplishment."

Elizabeth stared at him. "How—"

"Your teatime conversations with Miss Bingley and Mrs. Hurst have been endlessly entertaining."

She blinked in surprise. "You were listening?"

"Of course. It was by accident at first... but then I found that I could not deny the fact that I *wanted* to listen to your conversations."

"But those were *private*," Elizabeth spluttered.

"I daresay, Miss Bingley is not the most agreeable hostess," Mr. Darcy said, ignoring her shock. "But you rose to the challenge of her arguments and bitterness with an agility that I have come to admire—"

Elizabeth's chest tightened. This was too much. He should not have been listening... he should not be speaking to her in such a manner. What if someone overheard—

"Mr. Darcy this is most unexpected..."

"Is it?" he asked. "I should think that I am the more surprised party in this, Miss Bennet. As I told you in the garden, I have never allowed myself to feel anything for the young ladies I have courted—but you..."

"Mr. Darcy this is hardly the time—" Elizabeth's mind was reeling, and she was convinced that the other couples dancing nearby could hear every word that he was saying. She had not asked for this. She did not *want* it. How dare he—

"Miss Bennet, I do not know when *would* be an appropriate time," he said firmly. "All I know is the violence with which this affection has come upon me, and I fear that I shall go mad if I do not express it..."

"Then you shall go mad," Elizabeth hissed.

The last bars of the dance filled the air, and Elizabeth snatched her hand away from Mr. Darcy's grip and curtsied quickly.

Her face burned with embarrassed anger and her heart beat hard and fast in her chest. She had to get away from him.

Without waiting for Mr. Darcy to say anything, Elizabeth turned and fled the dance floor. She ducked through the crowd and did her best to lose herself in amongst the other guests.

Fresh air and time to think; that was what she wanted. But the thought of going out into the chill of the evening was less than ideal. She did not know where her shawl was, and it would be impossible to seek shelter elsewhere. She already knew that there were too many people outside—officers and gentlemen who had no inclination to dance, and the drivers and footmen who cared for the coaches and horses as they arrived.

As she exited the ballroom, she reached desperately for the knob on the first closed door, but it was locked. Elizabeth frowned and tried another door. Expecting the same result, she twisted the knob sharply and was surprised when it turned and swung open.

Elizabeth looked over her shoulder to be sure that she was alone, and then she entered the room and closed the door behind her.

She leaned against the door and took a deep breath to calm her racing heart. As her eyes adjusted to the dark, she realized that the room was lit with only the ghostly light of the full moon that hung overhead and shone in through the windows that looked out into Netherfield Park's extensive gardens.

The room was small, and octagonal in shape, and from the smell in the air, she could tell that this room had been, very recently, in fact, used as a gentleman's smoking room. The tables set for playing cards.

She should not be here.

Elizabeth sighed heavily and walked toward one of the couches. Perhaps if she could sit for a moment and collect her thoughts—

She seated herself on the couch and leaned back against the cushions. The upholstery was old and badly in need of repair, and Elizabeth wondered if Mr. Bingley had intentions of repairing or replacing the furnishings which had clearly seen too much use over the years.

She looked up at the ornately plastered ceiling and tried to organize her thoughts, but it was impossible to do so. "How dare he say such things?" she whispered. "How dare he presume..."

She had to stay as far away from Fitzwilliam Darcy as possible. She could not risk that anyone would discover what had just been said. If the gossips discovered such a thing—

Elizabeth groaned and rubbed her hands over her face.

"Miss Elizabeth Bennet... I was told that you had left the ballroom to take some fresh air, but I daresay you have gone the wrong way."

Elizabeth stood up from the couch with a cry of surprise on her lips. A tall gentleman was outlined in the doorway. Light from the corridor lamps spilled into the room and Elizabeth felt her heart squeeze uncomfortably in her chest at the sight of him.

"What are you doing here?"

"I believe that would be obvious, I followed you."

"Yes, but why?" Elizabeth said desperately. "Did anyone see you leave?"

"You would not speak to me, and I wanted to speak to you," he said simply.

"But, *why*? What else could you have to say that should require my presence?"

Mr. Darcy stepped closer to her, and Elizabeth became aware of the fact that he had closed the door, and that the only light in the room was the moonlight that spilled through the windows.

She needed to light a lamp.

This was... It was unthinkable... Impossible.

But more importantly: she could not be found here with him.

"Miss Bennet will you not hear what I have to say?" he said.

Elizabeth moved away from him and took refuge behind one

of the card tables where she fumbled for a packet of matches to light the lamp that stood upon the edge of the table.

"What could you *possibly* have to say that I would want to hear?" Elizabeth asked and she blushed at the tremor in her voice as she said those words.

"You did not allow me to finish. I meant to say that I cannot chase thoughts of you from my mind," he replied. "That, against my own better judgement, how much I needed to say aloud how much I ardently admire and... love you."

Elizabeth's eyes met his briefly before she focused on the matches in her shaking hands. "You are, indeed, mistaken," she said as she struck one and lifted the glass of the lamp to light the blackened wick.

The lamp flared to life and Elizabeth shook out the match before it burned the tips of her gloved fingers.

"Mistaken?" he said quietly. "No, Miss Bennet, I have labored under the delusion that I did not feel such things for weeks, nay, months, before I could finally admit to myself that it was true."

Elizabeth swallowed thickly and kept her eyes fixed upon the lamp. The glow of the shuddering flame helped her focus her thoughts, but her heart was beating furiously in her chest.

"But you have said yourself that such a thing is against your better judgement," she said boldly. "I do not know what you expect me to say in response. Should I thank you for such an admission. Should I be flattered that you have overcome your most sacred pride to deign to tell me such a thing?"

She could not keep the bitterness from her voice, and she did not care.

"You should not," he said. "In fact, I should be sorely disappointed if you did not argue such a thing with me. But I know now that I will never be happy if you deny me this. I will make you my wife, Elizabeth Bennet, and by God, you know that you cannot refuse me."

"I cannot?" Elizabeth scoffed. "You have a very high opinion of your offer, Mr. Darcy if you think that I would not refuse you in an instant."

"Would you?"

"I would," she replied.

"Marry me," he said softly and Elizabeth looked up at him in surprise. Her vision was blurred by the glow of the lamp and the darkness seemed sharper to her eyes. He was only half a step away from her. Close enough to touch.

She had not realized how close he really was.

"I—"

Elizabeth *wanted* to argue with him, and knew that she should have. But as much as he had complained about being unable to chase her from his thoughts, so *she* had experienced the same thing... Ever since their argument in the gardens of Netherfield Park she had been unable to do anything *but* think about him. He was arrogant. Impossibly proud. But to say that she truly hated him would be a lie.

She had hoped never to see him again, but that would have been impossible, and he seemed to relish that fact.

"What would you have me do, Miss Bennet?" He asked the question in a low voice that sent a pleasurable shiver up Elizabeth's spine. A shiver she could not fight. She should not have thought of him in this way. She should have done her utmost to push him away and forbid him from speaking to her...

"You should leave Hertfordshire," Elizabeth retorted. "Without a wife. I daresay it will not affect you in the slightest."

She did not know why she was so angry at him, but she could not help her ire. He did not belong here, and he had no right to make her feel the way she did.

"But, Miss Bennet, I am a terrible liar," he said. "Would you expect me to pretend that I will not pine for you? That I shall forget my offer of marriage?"

Elizabeth lifted her chin to look into his dark eyes. She could see the light of the lamp reflected in their dark depths, and something more, something that made her yearn to be held in his arms.

And then all at once, something inside her broke, and her anger toward him took charge.

"No," she replied firmly. "You do not need to forget. I *will* marry you."

Mr. Darcy blinked at her in surprise. "You will?"

His proposal had been terrible.

Insulting. Arrogant.

Almost cruel.

But her spite and anger was stronger than his attempts to bait her.

"I *will*," she said. "You have said, very clearly, that you love me against your will. I feel the same in that I feel that my affection for you has been cultivated against my own will. A misguided love. And so, we shall be miserable in our unfortunate affection for one another."

She closed the distance between them and pressed her lips against his, kissing him hard and brief before stepping away. She brushed her gloved fingers over her lips and glared at him.

"So, *husband*, we should make our announcement," she said.

"Indeed, *wife*," he growled.

A shiver rippled up Elizabeth's spine as Mr. Darcy extended his hand to her. She placed her fingers upon his palm and allowed him to lead her from the drawing room and out into the light of the corridor.

Applause and cheers rang out from the ballroom as they walked toward the door, and Elizabeth looked to Mr. Darcy in surprise.

"I see that Mr. Bingley's request for your sister's hand has yielded a positive result," he said dryly.

Jane... Mr. Bingley had proposed. How wonderful— Jane would be filled with joy and delight, and their mother would be impossibly proud... *and insufferable.*

"Then you will have time to decide how you will speak to my father about your own request," Elizabeth said tartly. "I daresay he will be in a jovial mood this evening; and you had best take advantage of it. But, pray, do not tell him that you love me against your will. I promise that he will not take kindly to such an admission."

Mr. Darcy's jaw clenched, and Elizabeth felt a small thrill of victory at making him angry. If he meant to go through with it, their marriage would be a bitter union, but one that he would not be able to walk away from easily. She would be sure of that.

7

"... And therefore is not by any to be enterprised, nor taken in hand, unadvisedly, lightly, or wantonly, to satisfy men's carnal lusts and appetites, like brute beasts that have no understanding; but reverently, discreetly, advisedly, soberly, and in the fear of God..." the priest's voice droned on and on, and Elizabeth found her mind wandering for the second time during the service.

It had taken very little time for their wedding to be planned, and Mrs. Bennet had finally gotten her wish that both of her eldest daughters would be married by the new year. A short engagement was all that Elizabeth could bear. While her sister had undertaken her vows with a look of unending love in her eyes as she stood next to Mr. Bingley, Elizabeth could not say the same.

She glanced at Jane and smiled to see how happy she looked. Jane looked radiant, her cheeks shining pink in the candlelight. Mr. Bingley looked as he ever did, pleasant yet mildly overwhelmed at everything happening around him.

Elizabeth felt a small swell of pride at the way the pearls in her sister's hair bands accentuated the hairstyle she had created.

They had helped each other dress this morning, and though both of their hands had shaken with nerves, they had been each other's comfort.

The chapel was filled with people, everyone that she and Jane had written an invitation to had made the journey to Netherfield Park, and the rooms at the inns in Meryton and houses nearby were all let.

Elizabeth did wonder how many of the assembled guests had come for the simple fact that they could say that they had attended a wedding where Lady Catherine de Bourgh was a guest of honor.

Except, Lady Catherine de Bourgh had declined her invitation. Even though she was now Elizabeth's aunt by marriage, she doubted that the woman would welcome her to Rosings Park anytime soon. Elizabeth stole a glance at the man by her side, he appeared stern and stoic as usual, but as she looked at him, he turned his head to meet her gaze and the smirk that twitched at the corner of his mouth filled Elizabeth with anger once more.

He knew as well as she did that this marriage was nothing more than a bitter experiment. She had lied to Jane about her intentions, and her declarations that she had, indeed to her own surprise, found the very deepest love she had always wished for.

She knew that she should have told Jane the truth, but she could not bear the thought that her sister might sacrifice her own happiness for Elizabeth's sake.

"I, Charles George Bingley, take thee, Jane Miranda Bennet, to my wedded Wife, to have and to hold from this day forward, for better for worse, for richer for poorer, in sickness and in health, to love and to cherish, till death us do part, according to God's holy ordinance; and thereto I plight thee my troth." Mr. Bingley's voice carried through the chapel, and Elizabeth heard a few of the ladies sigh as they remembered their own wedding days.

It was Fitzwilliam Darcy's time to speak, and Elizabeth turned toward him with her lips pressed into a thin line as he began to speak.

She barely heard him speak the words, all she could do was glare at him as his unwavering gaze held hers. Her hand was as steady in his as he slid the simple golden ring upon her finger. She swallowed thickly as the weight of the ring settled on her hand.

It was done. And she had no doubt that she was committing the most dire mistake in agreeing to such a union. But there was no way to reverse this arrangement. No way to undo what had been done.

As she had done on many occasions leading up to this moment, she cursed herself inwardly that she had been so rash in her agreement to his terrible proposal. She could not even blame the single glass of rum punch.

She should have told him to leave her presence. Told him that she despised him... anything but agreement to what he had offered. *Anything* but this.

But it was done.

And now she was Mrs. Darcy and Jane was Mrs. Bingley...

The smiling priest proclaimed them now happily wedded, and Elizabeth blinked, she had not heard the words, so lost was she in the moment. The smell of the herbs in her bouquet, the slight smile on her husband's face.

Her *husband*.

She hated the word.

Hated what it meant.

And what it would mean for the night ahead.

They turned together, she and Darcy, Jane and Bingley...

Newly wedded and pledged, they accepted the applause and good wishes of the assembled congregation.

Beside her, Jane's face was suffused with joy, and Elizabeth could only envy her sister's outpouring emotion. She could scarcely believe that such a day was possible, but not for the same reasons that her sister. It was difficult enough to stand there and keep her true emotions hidden, and Elizabeth was not entirely certain that she had accomplished such a thing successfully.

She looked to the man at her side, and fought against the urge to flinch away as his arm pressed against hers. She was Mrs. Darcy now, and as far as anyone knew, this man was her dearest love.

Luckily for Jane, Elizabeth was certain that her sister could not have found a better match in her own choice for wedded bliss. Despite her knowledge that Mr. Bingley had been in search of a bride for some time before happening to take an interest in Jane, he was a gentleman in possession of a pleasant and gentle nature which matched Jane's own, and Elizabeth could not be happier for her sister. Even if she had known of Mr. Darcy's deception from the beginning, it would not have made her turn Jane against Mr. Bingley.

Her sister was well matched in her partner, and while Elizabeth wished that she could say the same. She and Mr. Darcy were only well matched in their resentment for one another and the emotions that had so unwittingly consumed their better judgements.

The clouds overhead were fat with snowflakes, and as the newly wed couples climbed into the waiting carriage Elizabeth did her best to keep herself as far away from her husband as possible without alarming her sister to the fact that something was amiss. She had been able to distract Jane from any questions she'd had about how Elizabeth had felt about their approaching wedding, but Jane was observant, and if she were too overt with her reactions to Mr. Darcy's movements, Jane would surely suspect something.

A fur blanket was draped over their knees, and Elizabeth was grateful that it disguised how far away she had angled her legs from Mr. Darcy's.

The assembled guests left the chapel and followed the bridal carriage toward Netherfield Park and the lavish wedding breakfast that Mrs. Hurst, Mr. Darcy's sister, Georgiana, and the staff at Netherfield Park had seen to arranging. Caroline Bingley, who had sat sullenly during the wedding ceremony had also declined to be involved in the arrangement of the wedding celebrations, and Elizabeth could not help but wonder if the other woman had been disappointed by the developments of the past months.

Elizabeth was certain that Caroline had not expected that the Christmas ball at Netherfield Park would lead to a double wedding only a few months later.

"Are you cold, Lizzy?" Jane asked excitedly, her words interrupting Elizabeth's distracted thoughts. "We will be inside Netherfield Park soon, and I have been assured that everything is in readiness for our arrival. Mrs. Hurst and Miss Darcy have arranged every last detail." Jane's reassuring smile did little to calm Elizabeth's nerves, which were on high alert as her husband's thigh pressed against hers beneath the blanket. Elizabeth tried to smile as the carriage pulled to a stop in front of Netherfield's grand entrance.

Together, the couples climbed down from the carriage and walked through the great entryway and into the grand ballroom which had been set with tables and decorated for the wedding breakfast.

Crisp linens, crystal goblets, and hundreds of candles adorned the room, and Elizabeth's breath caught in her throat at the grandeur of the space. Mr. Darcy's hand pressed against the small of her back and she tried to move away, but could not do so before Jane and Mr. Bingley came up beside them.

Soon, this room would be full of their guests, and the Netherfield Park staff would bring tray after tray of carefully prepared dishes, candied fruits, and small cakes... they would be served wine, and sweet apple cider from the Netherfield cellars, and the celebrations would extend long into the night.

Perhaps the festivities would be drawn out long enough that they would be too exhausted to celebrate their union in the traditional manner.

Elizabeth had been dreading that eventuality, and she had struggled with the reality of her situation long enough that she had settled upon keeping her new husband as far from her bed as possible.

She could finally admit to herself that the prospect of her wedding night was terrifying, and she did not know if she would be able to get through the rest of the evening. She had not been able to speak to Mr. Darcy alone since that night at the Netherfield Ball, but she had come to several conclusions about what she wanted from this arrangement. He would have to agree to them, or she would not permit the charade to continue.

Their marriage might have been legal, but it was not real.

Elizabeth shoved her discontent deep down as the couples sat side by side at one of the long tables. Their guests, newly arrived from the chapel, flooded into the ballroom, exclaimed over the decorations, the beauty of the ceremony, and the generosity of their hosts. Elizabeth spoke quietly to Jane, but did not say anything about what was surely weighing on her sister's mind as well.

And that was what would happen when the last of the guests had said their goodbyes, and it was time to go upstairs... to bed.

The Bingleys and Darcys would be occupying Netherfield Park that night before Elizabeth and Mr. Darcy would depart north, bound for Derbyshire.

As the evening progressed, and not for the first time, Elizabeth found her mind wandering to the details of what lay beyond the doors of the bedchambers that had been prepared for them.

She only wet her lips with the wine, too nervous to drink, and she pushed aside the gorgeous food that had been loaded upon her plate by smiling members of Netherfield's staff.

From her seat at a nearby table, Caroline Bingley watched her with hard eyes, and Elizabeth tried her best to ignore the other woman's glare. Caroline's bitterness had tinged every moment of their interactions since the Christmas ball, but Elizabeth found it easy to push those tiny insults away from her thoughts. Caroline Bingley's opinion did not matter to her any more than it had when she had *not* been a married woman. In fact, it mattered less. Jane's position as mistress of Netherfield Park, and of Mr. Bingley's heart, could not be shaken now. Caroline could choke on her poison for all the good it would do her.

"Lizzy, are you not enjoying yourself?" Jane's voice was quiet, and Elizabeth looked at her quickly, pulled from her nervous contemplations of what lay ahead. Elizabeth forced a smile onto her face.

"Of course, I am having a wonderful time. This is more beautiful than I could have ever imagined. We must remember to thank Mrs. Hu— Louisa and Georgiana properly." It was proper for them to use their first names now... There was no need to be formal with family.

Jane returned her sister's smile and nodded emphatically,

but her eyes were on Lydia who sat with Mr. and Mrs. Bennet, and a red-eyed Kitty who looked as though she would burst into tears at the slightest provocation.

"Poor Kitty," Jane said. "She had been hoping to have her own engagement to celebrate after Mr. Harrison's interest in her at the ball. He even came to the house twice to visit with her…"

"Poor Kitty, indeed," Elizabeth said. It had been an unfortunate turn of events, they had all been very certain that Kitty would be planning her own wedding before the season turned.

Elizabeth gripped her sister's hand lightly and squeezed her fingers. It was obvious to her that Jane's concern for Kitty was merely a distraction from her own nervousness. Kitty would recover from her disappointment, and there would be a proposal waiting for her someday soon. Of that, Elizabeth was very sure.

Jane's smile wavered just a little, but Elizabeth knew that Jane was just as nervous as she, though for different reasons, and that gave her some strength.

The celebration continued late into the afternoon, and as the new brides were permitted to retreat to their bedchambers to refresh themselves, their guests were treated to a changing of the room, and the introduction of a group of players and musicians who distracted all assembled as the room was transformed into a ballroom once more.

Elizabeth parted from her sister after a quick embrace, and was directed to a room at the opposite end of the hallway by one of the maids.

A new dress had been laid out for her on the bed, and a bowl of steaming wash water was available for her use. Elizabeth sighed gratefully, dismissed the maid with a weary wave of her hand and steeled herself for the remainder of the evening.

Though the dancing and revels were supposed to continue late into the night, Elizabeth would have welcomed the opportunity to slide beneath the coverlet and allow sleep to overtake her.

Instead, she turned to the wash water and began to untie the ribbons at her shoulders to loosen the neckline of her gown. She was not expected to change quickly, but the sooner she returned, the sooner the evening would be over.

All at once, Elizabeth realized that she had not heard the door latch and she turned sharply toward it.

Mr. Darcy stood near the door, and a small smile played over his lips. "Shall I help you undress, Mrs. Darcy? Or will you be content to allow me to admire the view?"

She gritted her teeth as an enraged heat rushed into her cheeks, and she re-tied the ribbon at her shoulder with shaking fingers.

"Now, now, Mrs. Darcy, you cannot hide from me," he chuckled.

"I can, and I will," Elizabeth fumed.

The gentleman's eyebrow rose slightly as Elizabeth glared at him. "But I am your husband," he said, "would you deny me that which is mine?"

Elizabeth stared at him. "Yours?"

Mr. Darcy nodded and stepped into the room. The door swung shut behind him and Elizabeth swallowed thickly.

"You agreed to be my wife... There are certain privileges that come with such an agreement."

Elizabeth did her best not to step back from him, but it was almost impossible not to. "Agreement?" she snapped. She slapped away the hand that reached for her. "We made no agreement."

Mr. Darcy folded his arms over his chest and Elizabeth allowed herself to take a breath as he turned away and walked slowly across the room to the fire that burned in the hearth. "Perhaps we should."

Elizabeth straightened her shoulders as she watched him place another log on the fire. She had thought of this many times, but still did not know what she wanted. She had an idea... but did not know if it would be enough to guarantee that she would find any happiness in this... *union*.

She was miserable, and had every intention of punishing him, too.

"I am not your wife in anything but name, Fitzwilliam Darcy," she snapped. "If only to save another young woman from the bitter disappointment of your company."

Mr. Darcy laughed and straightened up from his task. "Do you doubt my love for you so entirely?" he asked.

Elizabeth shook her head. "I do not doubt that you have been tricked into this... affection by your own deeds. Your better judgement has been eclipsed by it, as has mine."

"Then you admit that you love me?"

"No," Elizabeth blazed, "only that I have also been tricked into this affection—" She bit her lip quickly to keep from saying anything more. She had not meant to admit such a thing. It was true, but she wished that she had not said it aloud.

"Your... affection for me," he said with a hint of a smile. "Indeed."

"Six months," Elizabeth said. "We shall *pretend* to be a happily married couple for six months. If, at the end of that time we discover that our unfortunate *affection* has been eclipsed by our good judgement, you shall..."

"I shall what?" Mr. Darcy asked.

Elizabeth lifted her chin and met his eyes boldly. "You shall buy me a house in London and never seek to share my bed again."

She had done it. She had made her demands.

He paused for only a moment. "I agree. But for those six months, you *will* be my wife," Mr. Darcy said. "If you refuse, I shall leave you on your father's doorstep, and you shall have to explain your presence there and *why* I have cast you out. Those are *my* terms, Mrs. Darcy," he said.

Elizabeth bit her lip briefly and her heart began to pound in her chest. The very thing she had hoped to avoid was being taken away; and she could not argue. If she refused, she would be shamed. Her whole family would suffer for her pride.

Her father might understand, but her mother—her sisters. *Jane.*

Such a scandal would touch all of them. Permanently.

"I agree," Elizabeth snapped.

Mr. Darcy smiled and Elizabeth's stomach tightened as he walked across the room and stopped in front of her. She stood still as he bent his head to kiss her, and even though Elizabeth tried to turn her head to avoid his kiss, he moved too quickly. His lips were hot and hard against hers and his hands were heavy upon her shoulders.

Elizabeth's hands came up to his chest, intent upon pushing him away, but as his mouth moved over hers, she found that her wish to escape his touch had been replaced by a very real desire to remain pressed against him.

Mr. Darcy lifted his head and looked down at her with a smile upon his face, one that Elizabeth was certain contained a hint of smugness. Her cheeks burned with shame at the way her body had betrayed her. There was no possible way that she could deny her desire for him.

"Leave me," she said breathlessly. "Our guests are waiting."

"As you command," Mr. Darcy said. His voice was husky and filled with desire.

Her heart pounded strangely as his fingers trailed over her collarbone, and when he stepped away the breath she took shuddered in her chest.

He left the room without another word, and Elizabeth was left with the disorder of her thoughts and the confusion of her emotions... did she hate him as she had tried to convince herself she did? Or was there something more—

Elizabeth rubbed her hands over her face and walked quickly to the wash stand. The hot water would help her wash away some of the confusion of what had just happened.

Mr. Darcy desired her, that was clear enough, but she would do anything in her power to keep him away from her bed.

Surely, the business of Pemberley would keep him occupied, and she could find more than one occasion to be too busy, or too exhausted to entertain his demands.

She washed herself quickly and pulled a new chemise over her head before stepping into the gown that had been laid out for her.

She bent to look into the mirror upon the vanity as she tied the ribbons at the shoulder of her new dress. Her eyes were bright and her cheeks were pink with the aftermath of her... victory. But could it even be called a victory?

Her cheeks were pink, and someone would surely remark upon the color in her face and neck, but she could easily explain it away as a result of the excitement of the evening.

Elizabeth re-pinned her dark curls and looked at her reflection once more before leaving the chamber to return to the ballroom.

Music filled the air, and the sound of laughter and conversation floated down the corridor. It was her wedding day, and she should have been as happy as her sister, but Elizabeth had other things upon her mind.

She and Mr. Darcy had made an arrangement.

Two, in fact.

But Elizabeth could not be certain of how her life would change in such a short amount of time. Six months could pass in the blink of an eye, or drag like the longest of summers.

If she was successful in keeping her feelings at bay, those six months of unhappiness would pass and Mr. Darcy would have no choice but to grant her whatever she wished. She would be free to do as she pleased in a fine house in London without fear of reprisal. But if she failed... If she gave in to her desires—

No. She could not allow such a thing to happen. And she would have to work diligently to keep him at bay without giving him cause to send her back to Longbourn in disgrace.

Would he do such a thing?

As she entered the ballroom, Mr. Darcy rose from his seat and smiled at her. Elizabeth's throat tightened briefly, and the heat in her belly flared once more.

If she gave in to her desires, he would win... and she did not know if she would be able to bear his smugness at such a victory.

Mr. Darcy came around the table and held out a hand to her. "Will you dance, Mrs. Darcy?" he asked.

"I could not refuse even if I wanted to," she replied. Her words might have been bitter, but her tone was not and Mr. Darcy dared to smile at her. Elizabeth allowed him to lead her to the dance floor and as the first notes of the dance rang out, she began to form a plan.

8

<hr>

*I*n the weeks and months that followed her wedding day, Elizabeth remained focused on the agreements that had been made in the bedchamber at Netherfield Park.

She and Mr. Darcy had returned to Pemberley soon after the wedding, but their marriage remained unconsummated.

As determined as she was to resist her desires, Mr. Darcy seemed unwilling to relinquish his request as well. They were both stubborn, but the strain was beginning to show.

Her husband was, as she had expected, preoccupied with the management of his estate. A business which had been neglected during his time at Netherfield Park.

He came to her bedchamber only once.

Elizabeth was awake, writing letters to her sisters by candlelight, but the door to her bedchamber was locked, and she did not look up when he knocked upon the closed door.

Meals were taken in the dining room, and to anyone who came to visit, including dear Georgiana who came to stay before leaving for Ramsgate once spring arrived, their marriage was as loving and uncomplicated as any other.

In polite company they talked and laughed together and

seemed to enjoy one another's company; but when they were away from prying eyes and behind closed doors their war would begin anew.

Elizabeth gave in to her desires in other ways, but her husband would never know of such things.

"Are you unhappy here, Elizabeth?" he asked her one evening over a dinner of roast pheasant that had been specially prepared for them.

"At Pemberley?" she replied innocently. "No. No, I am very happy here." She took a sip of her wine and looked at her husband over the rim of the glass. He had not touched his supper, though roast pheasant was his favorite dish.

"Are you unhappy with your decision to become Mrs. Darcy?"

"No," she said with a smile that felt more genuine than she had expected. "And when our arrangement is complete, I shall, indeed, be very happy."

Elizabeth knew that her words stung him, but she did not care. That is to say, she did not intend to care…

"Indeed. In a month our agreement will have been spent… and I shall buy you a fine house in London."

"I should like to be in Mayfair," Elizabeth said firmly. "As close to Hyde Park as can be managed. And I shall require a carriage, too."

Mr. Darcy's eyes widened. "Mayfair."

"Mayfair," Elizabeth repeated.

"I shall see it done," he said. "But under the terms of our arrangement, you do recall that you are, for all intents and purposes, under my command."

"Of course, Husband," she replied as she speared a piece of pheasant with her fork.

"My aunt has invited us to Rosings Park," he said.

"After so many months," Elizabeth laughed. "It is as though she were pretending that we were never married at all."

"I have written to tell her that we shall be happy to accept her offer," he said.

"Are we?" she asked. "Happy to accept?" The roast pheasant was richly spiced and she chewed with relish as her husband watched her.

"We are, Wife."

"Then it shall be a wonderful visit," she sighed and pressed her linen napkin to her mouth.

"Indeed," Darcy said thickly.

The six month façade she had agreed to would soon be over. *Would he allow it to expire without claiming her for his own?*

Her own resolve had wavered several times during the months she had spent at Pemberley, but she had not given in, and the door to her bedchamber remained locked.

You do not deserve his patience, a small voice whispered in her mind.

"We shall go to Rosings Park, as Lady Catherine commands."

Her husband nodded and plucked his wine glass from the table. He swirled the dark liquid in the glass and then raised it in her direction. "We depart in two days' time," he said. He drained the glass and set it down upon the table once more before he rose from his seat and nodded to her. "Goodnight, Mrs. Darcy."

His words were not stiff or angry, but she felt the sting of them nonetheless.

He strode across the room and left her alone with the remnants of the meal.

Elizabeth lifted her own wine glass and frowned at its contents before taking a sip.

"Goodnight, William," she murmured.

wo days passed swiftly, and Elizabeth saw very little
of her husband as he worked with the gamekeeper
and the gentleman who managed the business of the tenant
farmers. It was, indeed, hard work to keep an estate like
Pemberley running, and Elizabeth could not imagine the strain
that it must have placed upon him. In fact, she felt the sharpness
of regret that she had not taken an interest in the workings of
the estate.

In fact, the more time she spent at Pemberley, the more she
had to remind herself to push away her natural curiosity and
stifle her need to be involved in its functioning. She had not
asked Mrs. Reynolds for any keys, nor had she taken on any
meal planning or other duties that would usually be expected of
the mistress of such a house. She had left all of it to Mrs.
Reynolds. The housekeeper had not argued, but Elizabeth could
not ignore the older woman's cautious looks and could not
ignore the questions that lingered unasked.

Soon enough she would be in London, and all that would
matter was that her allowance would be paid, and that she
would have credit enough for new dresses and dinner parties
whenever she wanted them. Her friends could visit at all hours
of the day or night, and her sisters could come and stay with her
to seek their own independence in London. Mary, especially,
would benefit from such an arrangement. At least, that was what
Elizabeth expected would happen.

When Mrs. Reynolds came to tell her that the carriage was
waiting in the courtyard, Elizabeth was prepared for the
journey.

According to Mr. Darcy's plans, and her Ladyship's
invitation, they would stay at Rosings Park for several days, and

she could only hope that her husband would tire of his aunt's company in a shorter amount of time.

What little she knew of Lady Catherine de Bourgh did not give her confidence that the older woman would be supportive of her nephew's choice of a wife. But, she, herself, did not approve of their match, so her Ladyship's disapproval would not be unexpected or hurtful.

Elizabeth climbed up into the carriage and pulled a book from her valise to read on the journey. Mr. Darcy joined her shortly after, and the carriage pulled away from Pemberley with all speed in the direction of Rosings Park.

"There, Elizabeth, do you see it?" Mr. Darcy said as they turned onto the dirt road that led into the park.

Elizabeth set down her book and leaned forward to look out the carriage window to see what her husband was pointing at.

Rosings Park was a handsome structure that sat proudly upon rising ground. But Elizabeth was accustomed to the sight of Pemberley now, and in sharp contrast to that building, Rosings Park seemed to have been imposed upon its surroundings, and the many, many, windows which Mrs. Reynolds had taken great pains to describe in detail on several occasions served only to highlight the way the house appeared to loom over the surrounding landscape; dominating rather than complementing it as Pemberley did.

Elizabeth often wondered what the housekeeper's knowledge of Mr. Darcy's aunt's house meant, but she decided that she would wait to ask such a question.

"I do hope Lady Catherine will allow me time to change out of my traveling clothes," she said mildly.

Her husband murmured a response that was no doubt one of agreement, and Elizabeth tried to ignore the tightness in her chest as the carriage rolled past the white house and small garden that marked out the parson's house.

Her father had mentioned that his cousin, Mr. Collins, was under Lady Catherine's patronage at Hunsford, but though he would inherit Longbourn after Mr. Bennet's death, Elizabeth's marriage to Mr. Darcy had thankfully removed her need to associate with the gentleman. From her father's description of the parson, it was a happy development, indeed.

They were welcomed to the house by Lady Catherine's butler, a gentleman who looked very similar to Mr. Richards who cared for Pemberley alongside Mrs. Reynolds.

"Mr. Cotton has been in service at Rosings Park for nigh on forty years," Mr. Darcy said softly as they followed him down the corridor to the room they had been given for their stay.

Mr. Darcy left her there to prepare for the evening ahead while he went on into the house to speak to his aunt.

Though Pemberley was just as grand, Elizabeth did not feel comfortable at Rosings Park. The great house felt colder and more inhospitable. Summer was approaching quickly, but it did not seem that the warmth of the weather had managed to penetrate the walls of the house.

Elizabeth set her valise upon the bed and pulled out the clothing she had brought with her. She had chosen a pale grey muslin gown that would look very well in the candlelight that she had been told Lady Catherine preferred at her table, and a dusky pink ribbon to secure her curls away from her face.

As she dressed she thought about her husband, and the end of their arrangement. She had not expected six months to pass so quickly. Or so happily. Their arrangement had taken the bitterness from her approach to their marriage. She had expected to be angry every day, but such a thing was impossible, and her affection for Mr. Darcy, once an unhappy accident of her situation that had been turned into an act to be played in front of polite company, had become a very real thing. It seemed that lately she had found difficulty in summoning the cold and angry demeanor that had colored the first weeks of their union. Their interactions were pleasant, and they laughed often—something she had not expected from a man so stoic in nature.

But had she pushed her husband too far? Had she been unkind in her refusal to be a true wife to him?

Elizabeth heard the sound of the dinner gong as it reverberated through the house and waited patiently for her husband to come and fetch her for supper.

He arrived soon after, and offered her his elbow with the same smile he always wore when he escorted her to supper at Pemberley. It was painfully comfortable to lay her hand upon his arm and walk with him through the unfamiliar halls.

Lady Catherine's dining room was more formal than the one they used at Pemberley, and Elizabeth swallowed her gasp of surprise as they entered the room.

The glow from almost eighty beeswax candles lit the space, and though she loved the smell of the expensive candles, Elizabeth was struck by Lady Catherine's refusal to embrace more modern methods of lighting.

A large fire blazed in the hearth, and Elizabeth had no doubt that the room would be sweltering by the time dessert was served.

Another gentleman was seated at the table, and a young lady with a sickly countenance was placed near Lady Catherine's seat at the head of the table.

"My nephew did not tell me that his bride was related to my parson," Lady Catherine said by way of greeting. "Mr. Collins," she said to the dark haired gentleman, "were you aware that Mr. Darcy had wed your cousin?"

"Indeed, I did not know," Mr. Collins said. He smiled in a way that could only be described as desperately sycophantic and

Elizabeth was suddenly very glad that she had not met Mr. Collins in any other setting. This dinner would be quite enough.

Mr. Darcy pulled out a chair for Elizabeth and gestured toward the pale young woman across the table. "This is *my* cousin, Miss Anne de Bourgh," he said.

"A pleasure," Elizabeth said with a smile.

Anne de Bourgh said nothing, but only inclined her head slightly at the introduction.

"I had hoped that Fitzwilliam would see his way to marriage with my Anne," Lady Catherine said suddenly. She opened her napkin and spread it over her lap. "But he did not listen to *my* wishes. *Or* the wishes of his father..."

Elizabeth looked up at her husband and saw his jaw tighten as he pushed Elizabeth's chair toward the table and she offered him what she hoped was a reassuring smile as he took his own seat across from her. She had not known that he had disappointed many parties in his decision to marry her. She would have done him a kindness by refusing him outright.

Mild conversation accompanied the pouring of the wine, the majority of which centered upon Lady Catherine's complaints about the cold and her ill health over the winter months, which, she said, explained the need for a hot fire that evening. Elizabeth listened to all of it without making any comment of her own. There was no need for her opinions here, and there was no room for them, either.

Mr. Collins spoke of Hunsford, and made some mention of the entail upon Longbourn, but Elizabeth ignored his comments, too. Whatever disdain her father might have held for this gentleman, she knew it was warranted.

"Mrs. Darcy, I find that I know nothing about you." Lady

Catherine said loftily as the soup was served. "My nephew has been very careful with what he has told me, and I do not approve of secrets. So, I look to you for answers. Tell me of your family,"

"I..." Elizabeth did not know where to begin, and it was more difficult to do so when the table was filled with people who were watching her so closely. Mr. Darcy sat to the left of his aunt, and Lady Catherine's pale daughter, Anne, sat to her right. Mr. Collins was nearby, watching her every move. She set down her wine glass and folded her hands in her lap to steady herself.

"My family has lived in Hertfordshire for a very long time," she began. But she could go no further as Lady Catherine cleared her throat and interrupted her almost immediately.

"Ah, an old family," Lady Catherine intoned. "And your brothers and sisters?"

Elizabeth shook her head. "No brothers, your Ladyship, only sisters."

"And how old are they?" her Ladyship demanded.

"My youngest sister, Lydia, is seventeen this year," she replied. "Jane is the eldest. She was married to Mr. Darcy's friend, Mr. Bingley this winter. Lydia, Mary, and Kitty—Catherine—are still at home with my mother and father."

Lady Catherine blinked at her in confusion. "Five daughters... and all of them out in society?"

"They are," Elizabeth said with a smile. "It would have been impossible to keep Lydia at home during a Regimental Ball."

Anne smiled and looked down at her soup to avoid detection, but Elizabeth could sense that she had somehow already said too much.

"How disappointing for your father," Lady Catherine sniffed.

"I daresay," Elizabeth murmured.

Lady Catherine laid down her soup spoon and the footmen

who waited at the sides of the room sprang into action to take away the diners' plates, regardless of how much anyone else at the table had eaten. "And no proposals to speak of for the younger girls?" she asked archly.

"Not as yet," Elizabeth said.

"And what sort of amusement is there to be had in Meryton," Lady Catherine continued apace. "You made mention of a Regimental Ball—are there a great many soldiers in Meryton?"

"The militia keeps a garrison at Meryton," Elizabeth replied. "The officers undergo their training there before moving to Brighton for the summer months and then to their commissions."

"Green young men eager for battle," Lady Catherine said sagely. "I often scolded my dearly departed Henry for his fascination with the military. Too many foolish women have been taken in by a smart regimental uniform and a roguish smile." Her ladyship smiled thinly, but there was no mirth or joy in her face. "Are your sisters foolish girls, Mrs. Darcy?"

Elizabeth was not certain how to answer Lady Catherine's pointed and insulting question, nor did she know how to approach the judgement implied within it.

"I certainly hope not," Elizabeth said finally. "They are young, and inexperienced, this is true, but I do hope that they might know the difference between true happiness and compromise."

Silence fell over the table as the next course was brought into the room and Mr. Collins broke through it to explain to Lady Catherine his great plans for the expansion of the apple orchard that stood beside the parsonage.

Elizabeth, for her part, could feel Lady Catherine's stare burning into her flesh as Mr. Collins spoke exuberantly about the apple trees he wished to plant, but she refused to meet the horrid old woman's eyes.

Her comment about compromise had been accidental, but Elizabeth immediately regretted speaking those words. She could feel her husband's eyes upon her and the hypocrisy of it all burned in her mouth.

"If you will excuse me, I need to take some air," Elizabeth said. She pushed back her chair without waiting for permission to leave the table.

Mr. Collins choked on his words as she stood to walk toward the door, but Elizabeth did not pause to apologise or address the strange noises that were being made behind her.

One of the footmen opened the door for her, and she walked into the corridor with her shoulders back and her chin high. Perhaps after she was able to take a breath she would have been better equipped to face Lady Catherine de Bourgh's scrutiny, and the stares of the other guests at the table—but at the moment, she felt ill and sick at heart.

She strode down the corridor in search of a hiding place... Somewhere quiet that she could catch her breath and collect her thoughts. She had not been prepared for Lady Catherine's assault, Mr. Collins' presence, or the look that her husband directed across the table at her as she ate.

It was all too much.

A large door stood open and Elizabeth darted inside the room, only hoping that in a house with such famous windows that she would be able to find one that opened easily.

A library, softly lit with a fire set in the hearth filled her heart with relief and she closed the door just enough to give her some privacy.

She walked quickly to the bank of windows, pushed the curtains aside, and unhooked the latch to push the window wide.

The night air still held some chill, but Elizabeth was glad of it. She had been too hot in that dining room, and the fresh air that smelled of wet grass and apple blossoms was precisely what she had needed to help clear her mind. She closed her eyes and leaned against the window ledge. Only a few moments more—it would be worth the scolding she was sure to receive upon her return to the dining room. A few moments of solace—

The *creak* of the door hinge alerted Elizabeth to the fact that she was not the only one in the room and she turned in surprise to see who had followed her. She had expected to see one of the footmen, but was stunned to see, instead, that her husband stood in the room with her.

"You have a strange penchant for following me," she said mildly.

"Why did you leave the table?" he asked.

"It is as I said," she choked out. "I had need of some air. The conversation had become stale and I could not bear the pressure of keeping my opinions to myself."

He smiled briefly.

"I do enjoy your pert opinions, Mrs. Darcy," he said.

Elizabeth shook her head. *Why did he have to be like this?* He was so tall and handsome, insufferably so. His lips curved in a smile and Elizabeth felt her heart begin to beat faster in her chest.

"My aunt will not take kindly to both of us being absent," he said.

"Then why did *you* leave?" she asked angrily, but her ire was lukewarm.

"I gave another excuse as to my need to leave the party."

"I see," Elizabeth said.

She did not press for an explanation.

She did not want one.

She wanted him to leave her in peace so she could regain her composure and return to the table to face more of Lady

Catherine's arrogant questions with a grace and civility that the older woman did not deserve.

But he did not leave. Instead he stepped closer to her. "There is something else I wanted to say to you, Wife."

"Oh, indeed? And what could that be?" She could not hide the bitterness in her voice. This was not the time for such discussions, and she was not prepared.

"Our arrangement..." Mr. Darcy said gently. "It comes to an end in a few weeks time."

Elizabeth swallowed thickly. "You want to talk about this now?"

"The six months we agreed upon have almost passed and I have asked you this question before... Have you been unhappy at Pemberley?"

His dark eyes burned into hers, and Elizabeth felt a strange twist in her belly.

"I have been unhappy in our marriage," Elizabeth whispered. But it was a lie and now that he was here in front of her, her refusal to admit otherwise seemed hollow.

He was close—so close. Close enough to touch. Close enough to—

But she could think of nothing more as his arms came around her and pulled her against his chest.

"I think you are lying to me, Elizabeth," he said softly.

"I would never," Elizabeth gasped angrily. But it *was* a lie and her lips ached to feel his mouth pressed against hers.

As though he could hear her desperate thoughts, her husband bent his head and pressed his lips against hers. He was gentle, but she could feel an intensity behind the measured pressure of his mouth, one that she could feel radiating off him. His hands rose to her shoulders and his thumbs brushed over her exposed collarbones.

It was all so familiar, and she could not resist him. But he pulled his mouth away from hers and she felt heat rise in her cheeks.

How had she resisted those dark eyes?

They were full of passion and something more as he looked at her

"If you wish to return to your bedchamber, I will escort you there and give your apologies to my aunt."

Elizabeth laid a hand against his chest and nodded. Perhaps that would be for the best. The evening had not progressed well… and she did not want to embarrass her husband in front of Lady Catherine. Mr. Collins was another matter, but she could ignore him easily enough. Her Ladyship, however, presented a very different problem.

"And what will you tell them?" she asked.

Her husband took a breath and brushed his fingers against her cheek.

"I will tell them that you have taken ill. Her Ladyship sets a rich table, and it is easy to become overwhelmed by it. She will be flattered to hear me say such a thing, and will forget that you are not present soon after."

Elizabeth laughed softly and shook her head. "A most gracious hostess."

"The very epitome," Mr. Darcy agreed. "Shall I escort you to your chamber?"

He offered his elbow to her, and Elizabeth nodded and laid her hand upon it. She wanted to kiss him again, but he made no move to do so.

They walked out of the library and into the corridor together and Elizabeth leaned against him as they approached the door of the bedchamber she had been given.

"Where will you sleep tonight?" she asked.

Her husband's eyes did not leave hers. "Her Ladyship has

been kind enough to give me the use of my uncle's chambers for our stay. It is expected."

"Are they far away?" she asked.

His eyebrow rose. "Across the house."

Elizabeth nodded and removed her hand from Mr. Darcy's arm. She turned the knob and stepped into the room, but turned and leaned against the doorframe almost shyly.

"William—"

About to turn away, he paused. "What is it?" His tone was almost hopeful, and Elizabeth pressed her palm against her stomach in an attempt to calm some of her nerves.

"I wanted to tell you…" she said haltingly. "From the very beginning, from almost the first moment of our acquaintance, your manners, impressed me with the fullest belief of your arrogance, your conceit, and your selfish disdain of the feelings of others, were such as to form the foundation upon which succeeding events have built so immoveable a dislike that I could not now, nor ever, remove it from my heart."

Mr. Darcy frowned briefly and Elizabeth worried that she had gone too far. She reached up and placed a hand upon his cheek. "But I was wrong," she whispered.

The gentleman's jaw tightened and Elizabeth smiled. "What would you have of me, Mrs. Darcy?" he said softly.

"I would have you be my husband," she said simply.

Elizabeth's heart thundered in her chest as Mr. Darcy smiled at her. She had given in. He had won. And their agreement had ended.

"Tonight?" he asked.

"Every night," she murmured as he stepped closer. His hand fell to her waist and Elizabeth's eyes drifted closed as he bent his head to kiss her.

His lips were warm and yielding, but there was passion behind them, and his grip on her waist was firm and full of promise. Elizabeth pressed herself against him, her knees weak as she clung to his shoulders.

When he broke their kiss, he did so with a regretful groan.

"Shall we return to supper?" he asked gently.

Elizabeth smiled and felt the heat in her cheeks grow even hotter. "If we must."

Her husband chuckled and his arms tightened around her. "We must. But we shall not stay long here..."

"Is that a promise, Mr. Darcy?" She was teasing him now, and there was a spark of relief in his eyes as he looked down at her.

"Most assuredly," he replied with a smile.

The summer sun was warm upon her shoulder as Elizabeth stood at the edge of Hyde Park with her husband at her side.

"Mayfair," she said.

"Indeed, it is," Darcy replied.

"And this house?"

"It is yours, Mrs. Darcy."

It was a goodly house, to be sure. The door had been painted a dark green to match the ivy that climbed gracefully over the iron railing and up the side of the house. And it was hers, if she wished it to be.

But Elizabeth had not decided if this was what she wanted.

Not yet.

She had never been plagued by indecision, but in the final weeks of their agreement, she had proven to herself that such things required a great deal of consideration.

Their visit to Rosings Park had lasted only two nights before Mr. Darcy had made some excuse to his aunt about the need for their departure. Despite her questions, whatever that excuse might have been he would not tell her, and they had departed with all haste to Pemberley.

What had once been a facade of a marriage, was now a real one in every sense of the word.

Elizabeth was his truest wife, and what foundations had been laid in the first months of their marriage were brought to their fullest potential in those remaining weeks.

"Mine," she said as she looked at the front door and the winding ivy, but her voice lacked conviction.

Darcy seemed to sense her trepidation. "Shall we see what it has to offer?" he asked her.

"Yes," Elizabeth said hastily, grateful for the interruption of her confused thoughts.

They walked up the stairs together and Darcy opened the door so that she could step inside. The wide windows of the parlor allowed a good amount of light to enter the room and Elizabeth smiled to see how the main floor of the house was arranged.

"You may decorate it however you wish," Darcy said indulgently.

"I would not know where to begin," Elizabeth breathed, though that was a lie... In the first months of their marriage, she had planned every possible way that she would decorate the house she would be given as her reward for their bitter union, from the curtains to the table settings for the small dining room.

"Is it to your liking, Mrs. Darcy?" he asked as she turned in a circle in the middle of the room that would become the library.

"It is," Elizabeth replied happily. But her husband did not seem happy, quite the opposite, in fact, and Elizabeth laid a hand upon his arm. "What is it, William?"

"It is nothing," he said. "I have just been thinking of how quiet Pemberley will be when you are not there."

Elizabeth shook her head. "But why would that be?"

"You will move into this house, and I shall not see you unless we are commanded to appear as a couple... It will be as we agreed," he replied.

"Oh... But that would not suit me at all, Mr. Darcy," she said seriously.

He raised a confused eyebrow and Elizabeth smiled.

"As our old arrangements have been satisfied... I believe it is time that we make new ones. Do you not agree?"

Darcy blinked at her in surprise. "I— It would seem appropriate."

"I would not dream of leaving Pemberley without you at my side, my dearest love," she said. "Therefore, I propose that we leave Pemberley only when necessary—and we will come here, to London. To our little nest... To be alone together when the burdens of the estate become too much to bear."

Darcy smiled slowly, and nodded. "Our little nest," he repeated.

"But you must agree to include me in all of the business of the estate," she said firmly. "I have noticed that you labor far too much over your ledgers and accounts. I have decided that shall require some assistance. Especially when it comes time to make allowances for the children."

"The children..."

Elizabeth smiled. "Another agreement— One we shall have to speak of at length. In private."

"Elizabeth..."

"Hush," she said. "We have a great deal to discuss, and I should like to do it from a more comfortable location."

Darcy bent to press his lips to hers, and Elizabeth opened her mouth under his kiss and wound her arms around his neck.

It had taken her far too long to discover the truth of her

feelings for Fitzwilliam Darcy. A marriage that had begun in anger had yielded the very thing she had been searching for. The very thing she had begun to think was unattainable...

The very deepest love.

For he *was* her dearest love.

Though they had begun their marriage as adversaries, it had been revealed to her that not only were they well matched in wit and temperament, but also in their follies, and if that was not a sound basis for a marriage, then Elizabeth did not know how else she would prefer it to be.

THE END

ALSO FROM SOPHIA GREY

On a Winter's Star

A Missed Engagement

Unapologetically, Elizabeth

Officer Darcy

Elizabeth Abroad: France

Elizabeth Abroad: India

An Unexpected Joy

If I Were Mrs. Darcy...

Elizabeth's Deception

MERYTON MYSTERIES

The Trouble with Lords

The Trouble with Officers

The Trouble with Sisters

The Trouble with Engagements

The Trouble with Collections

www.ingramcontent.com/pod-product-compliance
Lightning Source LLC
Chambersburg PA
CBHW052050150726

48002CB00002B/828